HERE'S WHAT OTHERS ARE SAYING ABOUT KEITH A. ROBINSON'S ORIGINS TRILOGY

Logic's End is a great read, and I highly recommend it. It explores the question of what life would be like on a planet where evolution really did happen. The surprising result helps the reader to see why life on Earth must be the result of special creation. For those interested in science fiction but who are tired of all the evolutionary nonsense, *Logic's End* is a refreshing alternative.

—Jason Lisle, PhD, astrophysicist,
Institute for Creation Research

In this book, Robinson has discovered a "novel" way to communicate vital information to young adults and readers of all ages. Mainstream indoctrination on the origin of species and the age of the earth are regularly encountered, and has long needed combating. Through this unique story, truth is conveyed.

—Dr. John D. Morris President,
Institute for Creation Research

Pyramid of the Ancients will challenge you to reconsider the conventional wisdom concerning the history of our world.

—Tim Chaffey, writer/speaker,
Answers in Genesis, co-author of *Old-Earth Creationism on Trial*

Escaping the Cataclysm is an edge-of-your-seat thrill ride back through time. It brilliantly explains the plausibility of the Biblical account of history, especially Noah's Flood. It also explores details of the feasibility of the Ark itself and the Flood's impact on the earth. A great read!

—Julie Cave,
author of *The Dinah Harris Mysteries* series

Picking up where *Pyramid of the Ancients* leaves off, *Escaping the Cataclysm* hits the ground with both feet running. I found my faith renewed again and again as I was reminded of the many arguments that demonstrate why evolution cannot be the explanation for our origins.

—Joe Westbrook Co-author of *The Truth Chronicles*

DEHALI

TARTARUS CHRONICLES BOOK 2

DEHALI

KEITH A. ROBINSON

Cover Artwork by Jaslynn Tham
Book design copyright © 2015 by Tate Publishing, LLC. All rights reserved.
Cover design by Nino Carlo Suico
Interior design by Caypeeline Casas

Published in the United States of America

ISBN-13:978-1548275471
ISBN-10:1548275476

Fiction / Action & Adventure

Other novels by Keith A. Robinson

The Origins Trilogy

Logic's End:
A Novel about the Origin of Life in the Universe

Pyramid of the Ancients:
A Novel about the Origin of Civilizations

Escaping the Cataclysm:
A Novel about the Origin of Geologic Formations

To my children, Marissa, Tyler,
Alejandro, Joshua and Sebastian.
May you always hold strong to your faith
and keep God first in your lives.

Acknowledgments

I would like to thank my Savior and Lord. You are an amazing God!

To my wife, thanks for giving me the time to write. I know it can be lonely sometimes being married to an author!

To my editing team—Stephanie (my wife), mom, and Kevin (my brother)—thanks one more time for your help.

To my children, you all make me so proud.

To my cover artist, Jas Tham, you did it again! Thanks for sharing your talent.

To my fans, thanks for always encouraging me with your stories! It's what keeps me writing!

To my friends, and anyone else who helped me put this all together, thank you for your support.

CONTENTS

1 The Fringe 15
2 Svith Attack 24
3 Dehali 32
4 The Om Tower Hotel 42
5 Cautious Rendezvous 50
6 The Temple 56
7 Dark and Light 68
8 Plans 73
9 Connections 80
10 Sacrifice 88
11 Sarbjeet 93
12 Questions and Answers 102
13 Tact and Charm 112
14 Among Friends 123
15 Prometheus 130
16 Undercover 137
17 The Portal Opens 149
18 The Diversion 159
19 The Portal Readings 165
20 Surprises 170
21 Army of the Ahmed Caliphate 178
22 Exit Strategy 185
23 Aftershocks 192

24 The Untouchables 199
25 Revelations 207

Afterword 217
Suggested Resources 223
About Keith A. Robinson 225

1

THE FRINGE

The gentle murmurings of the flowing river failed in their attempts to soothe the tumultuous thoughts of the man sitting near the water's edge. His eyes looked up from the holographic screen hovering three inches above the small device in his palm. Lost in his thoughts, his gaze drifted over the dazzling veins of gold and silver that shimmered through the dark, purple-colored rock that composed the walls and ceiling of the underground cavern. The natural glow of the coral crystals that hung like small stalactites from the ceiling reflected off of the veins in the rock to create a dazzling display of shimmering light. However, the man's mind was too consumed by his thoughts to consider the beauty of his surroundings. Looking back down at the words on the holoscreen, he read them a third time, ingesting and dissecting each one.

The statement that "truth is relative" is self-refuting. If truth is relative, then the statement "truth is relative" is not true—it's relative! But to say "truth is absolute" would make perfect logical sense—because it is true that truth exists.

In the same way, there are many that say that matter is all that exists. But the statement "matter is all that exists" is not made of matter! It is a thought—a statement. Can matter explain the existence of a human soul? Can matter explain the worth of a human being? Can matter explain love?

Everything must eventually be boiled down to its ultimate reality. Either we are created by an all-powerful, transcendent God, or we are the results of the impersonal, random workings of matter—the Cosmos.

Since the major task of life is to discover the truth and align ourselves with that truth, we must take a hard look at the world around us and ask the hard questions to discover the truth. A few of the questions we must answer are listed below:

- *Is ultimate reality theism (the belief that there is a God outside of the universe who created it) or naturalism (the belief that natural causes alone can explain everything that exists)?*
- *Is nature all that exists, or is there also a supernatural realm?*
- *Is there a God who has spoken and revealed truth to us, or is truth something we have to discover, or even invent on our own?*
- *Is there an ultimate purpose to life, or are we just cosmic accidents?*

"Rahib!"

The voice broke into his reading with a thunderous crash, bringing the man back to the present. Although he couldn't immediately distinguish the speaker's identity, the use of his real name and not his chosen code name, Raptor, identified the speaker as his long-time friend.

"Over here, Caleb," Raptor called out, also choosing his friend's real name instead of his code name, Charon. Exiting out of the journal entry he had been reading, Raptor closed down the holographic reader and tucked it into his pocket. Turning at the sound of his friend's voice, the thick, muscular man redirected his nearly six-foot frame toward Raptor. His shoulder-length, stringy blond hair stood out in sharp contrast to his all-black ensemble consisting of boots, pants, shirt, and jacket. The disapproving frown on his friend's hardened features immediately caused Raptor's inward defenses to leap into place.

Since fleeing from Elysium six days ago, their friendship had become strained, due in large part to the fact that they now traveled with a rogue scientist, Gunther, and his cohort Braedon, in addition to their other two normal companions, Jade and Xavier. The fact that Braedon was a former government soldier and fellow protégé of Raptor's own recently deceased mentor, Steven, made matters worse. His affiliation with an underground organization known as Crimson Liberty added fuel to the already burning fire.

But Raptor knew that what really ignited Charon's hatred into a blazing inferno was the fact that Braedon was an unabashed Christian.

Although Raptor and Charon had been as close as brothers since their early teens, there were still many things about Charon's childhood that he had withheld. However, Raptor knew enough about the man to know that he despised all things religious. He felt it was a crutch for those who were weak and couldn't handle the brutality of life. He also felt it was a tool of manipulation that allowed spiritual leaders to justify their actions and exploit their adherents.

Up until a few days ago, Raptor would have mostly agreed with that assessment. But that was before Steven had given Raptor his private digital journal, which he had written to his wayward sons in the hopes of convincing them to return to his Christian faith.

Raptor *did* find the journal interesting and thought-provoking, but had he *only* read Steven's journal; he didn't think it would have impacted his beliefs much. But it *hadn't* just been the journal.

There had also been the prophecy and the two signs.

Just hours before his death, in a private conversation with Raptor, Steven had given him a cryptic prophecy that came supposedly "from God." It stated that only by "opening a door to a new life" would his own be saved. The second part of the prophecy stated that he only had thirty-one days to live, six of which had already passed.

Under normal circumstances, Raptor would have just dismissed it as the ravings of a lunatic. But circumstances had *not* been normal.

In addition to the prophecy, Steven also gave two signs to Raptor as proof that the prophecy was real. For the first sign, Steven described with disconcerting detail the dreams that had been haunting Raptor for some time, and which continued to haunt him still. The second sign was another prophecy that stated that God would miraculously spare Raptor's life before that day was through.

Raptor might have been able to rationalize away the first sign as being some kind of mental image planted in his brain via his electronic implant. But when his life *had* been miraculously spared from being sucked into the unstable portal created by the Vortex weapon, he knew there was more to this than chance and luck.

Someone—or something—was trying to get his attention.

Since the events of that day, Charon had also tried multiple times to explain away the signs. But despite his best efforts, Raptor's critical mind always discovered the hollowness of Charon's arguments. Their discussions had begun to cause a rift in their relationship, a rift that grew with each passing day and with each discussion.

The fact that Charon had come out to Raptor's secluded location himself instead of creating a Telekinetic Connection—or TC—through the implants meant he wanted to talk face-to-face.

"I figured you'd run off again," Charon said without preamble as he reached the rock on which Raptor sat. "I know that brush with death shook you up, but you're letting all that stuff with that so-called prophecy and those stupid signs rattle you. You need to be back at the camp, keeping an eye on soldier boy and his pet scientist. I'm tired of getting stuck babysitting while you run off and have your little…enlightenment sessions," he stated, doing nothing to hide the disgust in his voice and mannerisms.

Charon's mocking tone dredged up Raptor's own frustration. Standing up to his full six-foot, one-inch height, he met Charon's disrespectful manner with a steely gaze of his own. "I don't need you to tell me my responsibilities! I've been taking my fair share of turns watching them. What I do with my own time is *my* business!"

"That's fine, except that your idiotic, melancholy attitude is affecting everyone and making us all irritable," Charon shot back. "You need to get over this and move on."

"That's easy for you to say," Raptor said as he turned toward the river, his anger transforming into frustration. "You're not the one who has a possible death sentence hanging over you." Running his hand through his short cropped, jet-black hair, he let out an irritated sigh.

Charon's frown deepened. "I can't believe you still give that stupid prophecy any credence. Steven was just trying to manipulate you—"

Raptor held up a hand, cutting him off. "Just stop. I'm not going to rehash this with you again. You have your opinion, I have mine."

Swearing under his breath, Charon grunted and began walking away. "Yeah, well your opinion is full of *griblin* dung. All I have to say is if you keep this up, I'm outta here. And the others are likely to come with me."

Raptor stood in silence as his friend headed back in the direction of the camp. However, after taking no more than half a dozen steps, Charon froze mid-stride as a voice came through both his and Raptor's implants simultaneously.

Um, you two might want to quit splashing around in the river and get back here, **ASAP,** Xavier stated, a slight edge to his voice.

Tucking his portable holoscreen into his pocket, Raptor began heading back toward the camp at a jog even before he replied. It took a lot to shake the normally calm con artist. If he was unnerved, then something truly serious must be wrong. *What've you got, Xavier?*

Oh, nothing much, he replied sarcastically. *Just a pack of* **sviths** *heading right toward us.*

Charon, who had paused to allow Raptor to catch up to him, swore again as he fell into stride beside his friend.

Understood, Raptor replied as he quickened his pace. *Which direction?*

They're coming from both the north and the south, Xavier stated. This time, it was Raptor's turn to swear. With the river on the west and the cavern wall on the east, they were effectively trapped by the pack of vicious animals.

Wake up "the girls" and tell them to be ready. Charon and I will be there in a minute. Closing down the link between the mental implants, Raptor focused on running.

The moment he and Charon entered the edge of the camp, they could see Xavier, Jade, Braedon, and Gunther all running toward them. "They're almost here!" Xavier blurted out, glancing backward as they ran.

Assessing the situation, Raptor shook his head in frustration. "We'll never make it to the Cliffjumper in time," he stated aloud. He could already see the outlines of the creatures moving around the edges of the vehicle.

"How long before the group from the south arrives?" Braedon asked.

Raptor's eyes lost their focus as he used his implant to communicate with the tracker that was built into the vehicle's computer system. "Not more than two minutes at most."

"Will they damage the Cliffjumper?" Gunther asked, his panic rising.

"Possibly. It's been known to happen, especially if there's food in there," Jade answered as she reached up to her shoulder to lend reassurance to Zei, her pet *mindim*, which had perched there. The small, squirrel-like animal opened and closed its gray, leathery wings several times and let out a crisp chirp in agitation.

"Which there is," Xavier stated somberly.

"How many are we facing?" Braedon asked, his face set in determination.

"Eight near the Cliffjumper, and another ten coming from the south," Raptor said, his gaze locking with

Braedon's briefly before turning to the others. "Xavier, Braedon, and Gunther, head toward the Cliffjumper. See if you can distract those things long enough for Jade to get inside and get the engine fired up. She can then swing over and pick the rest of you up. Use the outside running boards and upper rail if you don't have time to jump inside. Charon and I will hold off the ones approaching from the south for as long as we can."

"What are these things?" Gunther asked as the others drew their laser pistols from concealment.

Raptor gave the older, balding man an impatient glare. With his gray fedora and matching suede coat, the scientist looked every bit as out of place as he probably felt. If it wasn't for the fact that the man was probably the only person in all of Tartarus who had the knowledge to be able to open the portals to Earth, Raptor would have left him behind long ago. Instead, he had to worry about protecting him. Although Braedon had taken it upon himself to begin training the scientist in basic survival skills, six days was not nearly enough for him to have learned much that would be of use in this situation.

"They are carnivorous reptiles about the size of a wolf and with a similar temperament," Braedon answered as he tossed one of his XR-27 laser pistols to Gunther. "They're kind of like a cross between a Rottweiler and a Velociraptor that runs on four legs."

Gunther swallowed hard at the description as he closed his hand nervously around the unfamiliar steel of the weapon. "I've…I've never heard of such a thing before."

"That's because they only live out here in the Fringe," Jade stated. "And they usually only attack people foolish enough to get too close to their nests."

"Or when they're really hungry," Xavier quipped.

"Save the discussion on *svith* behavioral patterns for later," Raptor snapped. "For now, we need to focus on survival. Let's move! Oh, and we'd appreciate it if you weren't late picking us up!" Raptor said as he and Charon headed off towards a large cluster of rocks.

"If we are, we'll make sure to bring mops and buckets," Xavier joked.

"Mops and buckets?" Jade asked, a disgusted look on her face.

"You know…to clean up what's left of them," he responded, a somewhat embarrassed look mixing with the expression of fear that was already in place. "Hey, cut me a little slack. The tension of the situation is throwing off my usual impeccable sense of humor."

By way of reply, Jade simply rolled her eyes.

"C'mon, let's go," Braedon stated as he headed cautiously toward the vehicle, his laser pistol leading the way.

2

SVITH ATTACK

As they drew nearer to the vehicle and what was left of their camp, Braedon watched as Jade silently headed off to the right, her pet *mindim* launching into the air and heading toward the ceiling of the cavern. Within a few moments, she had reached the rock wall on the east, her eyes never straying from the pack of *sviths* still intent on destroying the camp.

However, Braedon knew that they wouldn't stay that way for long. Because there was rarely any kind of breeze in the underground world to carry scents, most of the creatures hunted through other means. It wouldn't be long before Jade was discovered.

Crouching next to a large boulder, Braedon turned to his two companions to relay his plan when, unexpectedly, Gunther slid on a patch of loose gravel. Although he slipped only a few inches on the slight incline before regaining his balance, the surprising lurch caused a quick gasp to escape from his lips.

In unison, the *sviths'* pointy snouts angled toward the direction of the sound, the pair of twisted horns that grew out of their heads lowered defensively. Sighting the new prey, the reptilian creatures let out garbled, throaty howls as they leapt toward the group of humans, their toothy maws oozing yellowish saliva. In the semi-darkness of the cavern, the onlookers could see the streaks of red glow from between the blood-red scales as the creatures surged with energy and prepared to attack.

"You two stay here and cover me!" Braedon commanded. Bolting into action, he sprinted away from the boulder and ran toward another cluster of large rocks to the left, while simultaneously unleashing a barrage of laser fire toward the rushing animals. Taking the spot Braedon had just vacated, Xavier rested his arm on top of the boulder and fired his own shots toward the pack, one of which connected with the lead *svith* and dropped it to the ground.

"C'mon, old man!" Xavier yelled in frustration at Gunther. "Get over here and do something useful!" Trembling in fear, Gunther swallowed hard and did as he was told. Gripping the hilt of his weapon in both hands, Gunther aimed it toward the approaching animals and pulled the trigger, sending a wild blast of laser fire into the surrounding rocks.

Several yards to their left, Braedon had finally reached the cluster of smaller rocks and began focusing his attention on slowing the oncoming assault. Between the three men, they were able to bring down several more of the creatures before the animals were within striking distance. However, the loss of their companions didn't serve as any kind of deterrent to the three remaining *sviths*. As the animals closed the gap, they veered away from Xavier and Gunther and headed directly toward Braedon.

Bracing himself for the attack, Braedon lowered his weapon and fell into a fighting stance just as the first beast leapt. Only his years of training kept Braedon alive. Dodging to the right at the last second, the soldier used his left arm to push against the animal's body, causing its fangs and claws to miss their mark. A few steps behind the first, the second *svith* quickly altered its course toward Braedon. Instead of dodging this attack also, he rolled backward and planted his foot into the creature's stomach as it charged. Using its own momentum against it, Braedon continued his roll and kicked, sending the animal flying in the same direction it had currently been traveling.

However, the maneuver left Braedon facedown on the ground and open to the attack of the third *svith*. Before he could regain his fighting stance, the last beast jumped on his back. He instantly twisted his body to his left, narrowly avoiding the creatures' jaws as they attempted to snap down on his leg. Although the movement caught the animal off guard, it quickly recovered and used its considerable weight to pin Braedon on his back. As the *svith* lunged toward his face, Braedon managed to bring his left forearm up in time. A blinding flash of pain shot through his arm as the serrated teeth sank into his flesh. Fighting against the blackness that sought to claim him, he brought his right arm up, placed the nozzle of his pistol against the creature's side, and pulled the trigger.

Instantly, the vice-like pressure on his arm ceased. Pushing the dead creature off him, Braedon tried to focus on the two remaining reptiles that had recovered and were even now preparing to attack. Just then, several laser blasts flew past his head and into the creatures.

"Braedon," Xavier said as he reached the soldier's side. "C'mon! Jade's got the Cliffjumper ready, but Raptor and Charon are in trouble." Fighting his dizziness and cradling his injured arm, Braedon allowed Xavier and Gunther to help him to his feet. As quickly as possible, the three men crossed over to where Jade had the vehicle idling several feet away, the side door open and ready to receive them.

"Move it!" Jade commanded, her voice strained. Beside her, Zei chattered noisily from where it stood on the passenger seat.

The moment the last of the men were inside, Jade punched the accelerator, sending the large, hovering vehicle lurching forward.

Brushing the chattering *mindim* out of the way, Xavier climbed into the passenger seat beside the woman. "Where are they?" he asked, his normally handsome features lined with worry.

"I don't know!" Jade replied. "They were over on that ridge a few moments ago."

"Look!" Xavier said, pointing. "The rest of the *sviths* that came from the south are over by the bank of the river!"

Jade cast Xavier a frantic look. "You don't think they'd be stupid enough to…"

"They must have!" Xavier stated.

Grabbing the steering wheel firmly in hand, Jade pulled it hard to the right and sent the vehicle careening over the short cliff toward the river. Instantly, the vehicle's repulsors sent water spraying out in all directions. Once the Cliffjumper had stabilized, Jade sent it forward as quickly as she dared, headlights illuminating the turning water.

"There!" Xavier shouted in excitement as two bobbing forms became visible at the edge of the vehicle's beams.

Jade swore softly, dread permeating her voice.

"What is it now?" Gunther called out as he leaned forward to peer out the front window to see a bright green glow traveling rapidly through the water toward the two floundering men.

"A school of Razor Fish," Jade stated. "And they're closing in fast. Xavier, I'm gonna make a flyby on their left. You've got one chance, pretty boy. Don't miss."

Nodding nervously, Xavier turned in his seat to look at the two men behind him. "Gunther, grab the synth-rope extender out of the compartment behind you. Braedon, open the side door and be ready. Braedon, do you hear me?"

Although pale from loss of blood, Braedon readied himself and opened the door, determination and adrenaline commanding his actions. Shaking from fear, Gunther finally retrieved the cylinder of synth-rope and handed it to Xavier.

A moment later, Jade expertly maneuvered the Cliffjumper alongside the drowning men. The spray from the vehicle's repulsors, however, made it impossible for her to get closer than ten feet from them. As she stabilized their position, she noticed with concern that while Raptor was fully alert, Charon appeared lethargic and barely conscious.

"Now!" Jade shouted.

Xavier pointed toward Raptor's outstretched hand and pressed the release button. Immediately, a coil of thin, rope-like material shot out of the end. After a couple of failed attempts, Raptor's hand finally closed on the synth-rope. While still fighting to stay afloat, Raptor took the end of the rope and wrapped it around Charon's upper torso, all the while trying to ignore the green glow that was now only a dozen feet behind them. His task complete, Raptor gave a weak tug on the rope, which Xavier had now secured to the frame of the Cliffjumper.

Instantly, Xavier, Gunther, and a weakened Braedon began reeling in their catch. Blinded by the spray from their vehicle, the men reached out and grabbed the outstretched arms of their floundering companions. Then, just as they began pulling them inside, Raptor and Charon began to scream. The sound of the men's agony fueled the strength of their rescuers. Within moments, the two men were aboard. However, attached to their legs were several fish about eight inches in length with bright green scales.

"Get 'em off!" Raptor cried out in panic.

Xavier and Braedon immediately set to work, carefully extracting the carnivorous fish and tossing them back into the river. Within moments, Jade had the Cliffjumper off of the river and safely traveling once more on solid ground. For several seconds, no one spoke, each lost in his or her own thoughts of what might have been.

"Charon…" Raptor wheezed, finally breaking the silence. "He's…he's injured."

"Xavier, Gunther, out of my way," Jade commanded as she turned on the vehicle's computerized driving program and vacated the driver's seat. Doing as they were told, the two men moved to the back of the vehicle to give Jade room to examine her wounded comrade.

"What happened?" Jade said as she carefully removed the large man's shredded jacket and examined the deep slashes in his back.

"Charon and I took out several of the beasts, but the pack quickly gained ground on us," Raptor said as he propped himself into a sitting position on the floor. "We knew you wouldn't get to us before they did, so we started heading toward the river. However, a couple of the *sviths* managed to catch us just before we dove into the water. One of them raked Charon with its claws pretty bad before I shot it."

"He's going to need professional medical attention to stitch up these gashes," Braedon stated.

"As do you," Gunther said from the back seat. "I thought for a second that creature was going to bite your arm clear off."

"Fortunately, we're less than a day from Dehali," Raptor said. "Xavier, take the driver's seat. Head back toward the main road and get us to the city as quickly as possible."

"The main road?" Xavier said hesitantly. "But…I thought the whole point of driving through the wild parts of the Fringe was to avoid notice from the Elysium Security Force. In case you forgot, they're still ticked off at us for sneaking out of the city with their secret Vortex weapon!"

Raptor shot the man an impatient look. "It's a risk we'll have to take. Charon's lost too much blood already. Now go!"

Swearing under his breath, Xavier climbed into the driver's seat. A moment later, Raptor made his way stiffly to the passenger seat. Brushing aside Jade's pet *mindim* who had taken up residence there once again, he sat down heavily into the seat. Chattering at the man indignantly, the creature scurried across the floor of the vehicle toward its master, who was busy dressing Charon's wounds with the medical kit. Once Jade had finished and made sure Charon was resting comfortably, she turned her attention to the deep bite marks on Braedon's arm.

"I don't understand something," Braedon said, wincing in pain as Jade bandaged his arm. "From what I'd heard, *sviths* aren't normally in this section of the Fringe. What would force them to travel so far from their dens?"

"I don't know," Raptor replied. "But it doesn't bode well. Anything that can chase out a large pack of *sviths* is nothing to mess with. If something is throwing off the ecological balance out in the Fringe, it could make traveling between the larger cities more dangerous. We'll definitely have to keep a tighter watch."

An ominous silence settled over the group, causing Xavier to turn on the Cliffjumper's digital music player. Despite the blaring music, no one in the group succeeded in shaking off the disturbing thoughts conjured up by Raptor's last comment. It appeared that unsettling events weren't just taking place in the city of Elysium. Something was going on, and each of them secretly wondered if there was anywhere in the entire underground world of Tartarus that wouldn't be affected.

3

DEHALI

"We're almost there," Xavier announced as he steered the Cliffjumper into the flow of other vehicles traversing the highway. Since the incident with the *sviths*, the group had traveled without incident for over sixteen hours, stopping only to refuel and eat. During that time, Charon's condition continued to worsen. Although Jade's medical ministrations had succeeded in stabilizing him somewhat, he grew weaker and weaker with each passing hour.

Ahead of them, the ceiling sloped gently upward, indicating that they were entering the outskirts of the enormous cavern that housed the city of Dehali. In addition to the natural indicators, the ground beneath them transitioned from reinforced rock to the high-tech digital roadways that covered the entrances to each of the major cities of Tartarus. Each city sought to outdo the others by customizing the patterns and colors used on the roads. In this case, the planners of Dehali decided to use broken gold-colored lines between lanes and bright orange on the outermost ones.

However, most of those traveling on the roads paid little attention to the color of the lines due to the fact that their attention was instantly captured by the colorful holographic displays that assaulted them on all sides. Traffic patterns, exit routes, and pertinent information were displayed at regular intervals on the ceiling and moved in the direction of the travelers at slightly slower speeds, making them easier to read.

Following a similar setup, digital billboards moved along slowly on each side of the roadway, presenting to visitors three-dimensional images of the vast array of attractions and entertainment to be found in the city. The entire panorama was so overwhelming to many drivers that the digital roads were lined with sensors that communicated with the onboard computers of the vehicles to make sure their drivers didn't veer out of their own lanes.

"Hey look, Charon," Xavier said cheerfully. "Your favorite musical's in town! *Legends of Love,* starring Dadhija Johar. Oh, hey, that's new!" he exclaimed. "I just received a TC message that says, 'This show utilizes implant technology to create a truly immersive theatrical experience!' Doesn't that sound fun?"

Glancing over his shoulder and seeing the pale, comatose complexion on the big man's face and the worried expressions on the faces of the others, Xavier sighed and focused on his driving, the humor failing miserably to cut through the tension in the vehicle.

"Okay then," he muttered under his breath. "Maybe next time."

"This is incredible," Gunther stated softly, his eyes fixed upon the images. "I've never seen anything like this."

"Yeah, they can certainly put on a show of civility and grandeur," Braedon said. "Elysium's main entrance has an even more impressive show. With us taking the back door out of the city, you missed all of the pizzazz." He paused, his features hardening. "But the sad part is that the glitz and glamour only serve to hide the rotten core. Most of this fancy entertainment that is being advertised here is reserved for the wealthy upper castes. Those who live in the lower two levels of the city struggle just to survive. Many of the poorest live in complete squalor or filth."

"Lower two levels?" Gunther repeated. "What do you mean?"

"See for yourself," Braedon replied, pointing toward the front of the vehicle.

As Gunther peered out the window, the ceiling and walls appeared to fall away into the distance as the cavern opened wide to reveal a magnificent cityscape. The city consisted of four distinctly separate sections. The main highway on which the Cliffjumper traveled led directly into the lowest of the four sections. To the left of this level, and nearly six stories higher, was the second section. Further back and another six or seven stories higher was the third portion of the city. The highest and top level was far off in the right corner of the immense cavern.

The wonder of the city was enhanced by a series of majestic waterfalls that began from behind the uppermost level and cascaded down from each section of the city. Upon reaching the lowest level, the waters merged to become a river that flowed around the western side of the city.

Taking advantage of the natural beauty, craftsmen erected a series of elegant bridges that crisscrossed the waterfalls and connected each of the upper three levels to the one immediately beneath. In addition, a single, long, winding bridge split off the main thoroughfare and traveled along the edge of each of the levels, ending at the topmost section. Exit ramps connected the bridge to each portion of the city, allowing those doing business to bypass the lower levels entirely. Along the cliff edges of each section, repulsor lifts of various sizes could be seen transporting vehicles and goods up and down between the levels.

But the most spectacular part of the entire scene was not the city itself, but the source of light that bathed the whole city in soft, golden hues. Veins of what appeared to be molten gold ran throughout the walls and ceiling of the cavern like the many strands of a spider's web. Each of the jagged lines glowed brightly, casting its pulsating light down upon the citizens below.

"Is that…is that a natural formation or…?" Gunther stammered.

Despite having been to Dehali on several other occasions, Braedon nevertheless found his own gaze transfixed upon the city. "More or less," he answered. "The structures are natural, but the founders of the city discovered that by applying various amounts of electricity to the walls of the cavern, they could control the amount of light given off. So during the 'day,' they amp up the power, and at 'night,' they let it dim significantly. It helps to regulate the sleep cycles of the citizens."

"And it allows some of the more…colorful…personalities a chance to come out and do business," Raptor added from where he sat in the front passenger seat.

Ignoring the comment, Braedon continued, "Whether this entire cavern formation is natural or partially manmade is uncertain. Regardless, the founders used the setup to reflect the four ancient social groups, or *varnas* as they're called. Each of the *varnas* have specific Hindi names that I don't remember, but they are broken down sort of by occupation: the priests, the nobles and warriors, the workers—farmers, craftsmen, etc.—and the unskilled laborers. Nowadays, the four *varnas* have been broken down into thousands of groups called castes."

"But I thought the caste system was abandoned in India years ago on Earth," Gunther said. "Why would they bring it back here?"

"Old habits and ways of thinking die hard. Especially *religious* ways of thinking," Raptor stated derisively.

"From what I understand, although the caste system was *officially* dissolved by the government, it's still important to the Hindu people and is recognized as the proper way to stratify society," Braedon said. "So when the first settlers arrived here from Earth, they reinstated the caste system to help organize the new society. The call to remove the system is gaining ground, but not only do opponents have to fight old traditions, they also have to work against the very layout of the city."

At that moment, Charon stirred and coughed. Xavier chuckled. "I agree with Charon's assessment of this conversation."

Reaching over, Jade checked Charon's vitals quickly and glanced toward Raptor. "His pulse has dropped slightly."

Raptor merely nodded, his expression neutral.

"Where do you plan to take him to get medical attention?" Braedon asked. "I'm assuming you won't be taking him to a hospital."

"Why not?" Gunther asked, his voice low so as not to make the others aware of his ignorance.

"Too easy to trace," Braedon stated casually, his attention still focused on waiting for Raptor's reply.

Gunther nodded in understanding as Raptor responded.

"We've got some friends that we've worked with in the past who can help us," he said. "It won't be the best care money can buy, but I trust their skills and their ability to keep their mouths shut."

"Which level of the city?" Braedon inquired further as Xavier guided the Cliffjumper onto the long winding bridge that led to the upper sections.

"The third."

Letting the conversation drop, Braedon turned his attention to the window, where Gunther was staring in unabashed fascination at the city. "Do you see those buildings with the roofs that look almost like tall steps? They're everywhere in the city, but especially near the waterfalls, the river, and the cavern walls. Are those temples?"

"Yeah," the soldier replied. "Each one is dedicated to one or more of the three hundred and thirty million gods and goddesses they worship."

"Three hundred and thirty million!" Gunther repeated in shock. "I knew they had a lot of gods, but I didn't realize they had *that* many."

"The reason for the high number is that Hinduism is basically a pantheistic religion," Braedon explained as the Cliffjumper passed the first exit ramp and continued on toward the one that would take the group to the third level. "They believe that god is everything and everything is god. It's kind of like the Force from those old *Star Wars* classics. This includes the rocks of the cavern, the plants, animals, humans, you, me...everything."

Xavier snorted from his place in the passenger seat. "I've met several people who *think* they're God. Just take our 'beloved' governor of Elysium, Mr. Devyn Mathison. If anybody thinks he's God, that guy sure does."

Braedon harrumphed in agreement. "But there's a big difference between *thinking* you're God and actually *being* one. Then again, Hindis use the word god to mean something different than monotheistic religions. When we think of God, we think of a being with a will and personality who can make choices and act upon those decisions. But the Hindu concept of God is more generic than that. It simply means that everything that exists is a part of this ultimate reality, or Brahman.

"The most common legend or analogy is about a wise man who taught his son about Brahmin by putting some salt into water and asking his son to take it out again," Braedon continued. "Of course, this was impossible because the salt dissolved. Supposedly, the man equated the presence of Brahmin to the salt in the water: invisible but everywhere."

As Xavier turned the vehicle onto the exit ramp leading to their destination, Gunther turned away from the window to look at Braedon, a confused expression on his face. "So how do the three hundred and thirty gods fit with Brahman?"

"They are supposedly all different aspects of Brahman," Braedon said. "I don't understand it completely myself. If Steven were here, he could explain it much better. He loved studying this kind of stuff."

"Sorry to break up the humanities lesson, but we're almost there," Raptor said matter-of-factly. "As soon as we stop, I'm going to need Xavier, Jade, and Gunther to help me get Charon inside."

Conversation in the vehicle ceased as Xavier deftly navigated slowly down the busy roads of the city. People filled nearly every inch of the city streets. Many were occupied with buying fruit, flowers, and incense from the local vendors, while others stood near shrines located on the street corners. Holy men sat in yoga positions near the shrines chanting softly and fingering beads while the crowds passed by.

Despite the fact that much of the city was filled with advanced technology, much of the population still chose to dress in traditional Hindi garb. Black and red dots adorned the foreheads of many of the women, and a few even carried baskets on their heads.

As the Cliffjumper passed one of the temples, Gunther noticed that both men and women were removing their shoes before entering. Furthermore, many of the women were covering their heads with colorful and decorative scarves before stepping into the building.

However, before Gunther could ask Braedon about the practice, Xavier turned the vehicle onto a narrow street and brought it to an abrupt stop in front of what appeared to be a small medical clinic. Within moments, Jade had the side door open and was beckoning for Gunther to move into position. Wincing in pain as he moved his injured arm, Braedon stepped out of the vehicle and began casually perusing the area to make sure no one took any particular interest in the activities of his companions.

Before long, Raptor, Xavier, Jade, and Gunther had Charon out of the vehicle and up the short steps leading to what appeared to be a modern medical clinic. The moment the group entered the main lobby, several clinic workers eased Charon into a wheelchair and took him through a set of doors with Raptor and the others walking close behind.

"Raptor, it's good to see you." The thickly-accented voice came from a middle-aged man dressed in modern office attire underneath a white lab coat. He and Raptor shook hands as a nurse approached Braedon and began examining his arm. "You all look like you just got into a fight with an angry *tunrokla*. What happened?"

"A pack of *sviths* decided they liked our camp and wanted to move in."

"*Sviths?*" the man repeated. "That's odd. What are they doing so close to the city?

"We were asking the same question," Raptor said. "One of them tore up Charon pretty good with its claws. Thanks for your help, Janak. I owe you one."

"We'll take care of him, and your other friend's arm," Janak stated as he gestured toward a room off to his right. "You and the rest of your group can wait in here. I'll be back momentarily with an update on Charon's condition."

"Actually, I could use a little help as well," Raptor stated. "We had a little run-in with a school of Razor Fish as well. Most of the bites are superficial, but…"

The other man raised an eyebrow curiously as he studied not only the cuts from the fish, but the old laser wound on Raptor's left shoulder as well. "*Sviths,* and Razor Fish, huh?"

Despite himself, Raptor couldn't help but grin. "Yeah, well, the creature that gave me *that* particular wound was wearing an ESF uniform."

"I see," the man said knowingly. Janak held up a hand, stopping him midsentence. "It's a good thing you were wearing your *svith*-scale jacket or your wounds would have been worse. Come with me, and we'll get *your* wounds treated as well."

As Janak headed off with Raptor through a nearby door, Jade, Xavier, and Gunther stepped through the door that Janek had indicated and entered into the simply-furnished side room. Gunther sank into one of the plush chairs that sat along the walls of the room, while Jade leaned against the far wall where she had a clear view of the door. Xavier, on the other hand, strode purposefully up to the nearest vending machine and purchased several snacks. Grabbing his newly acquired junk food, he stepped over to one of the other chairs and sat down. For several minutes afterward, the only sound in the room came from Xavier as he munched greedily.

Finally, after the better part of a half hour, the door to the room opened, and Raptor stepped in. Even before the door had finished closing behind him, Jade stood fully upright and asked, "Are we going to wait for word on Charon, or do we leave now?"

Raptor, still shrugging off the after affects of the clinic workers' ministrations, paused for a moment before responding, "Janak has an implant, so he can contact me with word on Charon. I don't think we should waste any more time." Turning his gaze upon Gunther, he said, "Well, Professor, what do you say we go find out if your old friend Travis followed through on his promise. We leave immediately for the Om Tower Hotel."

4

THE OM TOWER HOTEL

Although most of the architectural style of the Om Tower Hotel was modern, remnants of more ancient styles, such as domes and arches, could be seen on the roof of the enormous building. Made of a type of reflective material, the outer walls, pillars, and roof seemed to dance with light from the shining veins of gold coming from the distant cavern walls and ceiling. Located in the center of the uppermost level of the city, which consisted mostly of the Brahmin caste of priests, artists, and scholars, the Om Tower Hotel was one of the most exquisite and refined buildings in the city.

The small, sleek hovercar drove casually down the extended driveway and past the carefully manicured lawn containing numerous statues and fountains until it pulled up to the entrance of the hotel. As the solid black vehicle came to a stop, a middle-aged Caucasian man stepped out of the passenger side door, a dark-brown briefcase in his right hand. Closing the door behind him, the man turned around and studied his reflection in the dark glass of the car. After rubbing his hand over his bald head, he adjusted his glasses and stroked his sandy-blond, neatly trimmed beard and mustache. Taking a moment longer to adjust his silver-streaked tie and dark, pin-striped business suit, he turned around and strode through the entrance of the hotel as the car accelerated and headed back down the driveway toward the main flow of traffic.

Walking casually into the foyer of the hotel, the man took a moment to admire the elegant tapestries and statues of the various avatars or incarnations of the Hindu deities that were placed along the walls. Although he found these fascinating, his attention was quickly drawn to the three ornate, life-sized statues that were placed on pedestals at even intervals throughout the large, rectangular room. The statues were of the three primary representations of the supreme Brahman: Brahma the creator, Vishnu the preserver, and Shiva the destroyer.

After taking several minutes to study the craftsmanship of the building's decor, the man stepped past two men sitting on a nearby couch and casually stepped up to the concierge's counter. While he waited for the employee to finish his implant conversation, his gaze rested upon the nearly wall-sized tapestry that hung behind the counter just under the words: The Om Tower Hotel. The tapestry consisted of a single symbol, surrounded by a sea of blue, with a border of swirling shades of red, yellow, and gold. Inside the symbol, depictions of Brahma, Vishnu, and Shiva could be seen, each woven expertly into the cloth.

"Welcome to the Om Tower Hotel. How may I help you?" the concierge said in thickly-accented English, pulling his customer's attention away from the tapestry.

The visitor smiled warmly in return. "This is quite a place you've got here. I am particularly enraptured by the beauty of your murals and statues. What is that symbol on the tapestry behind you?"

"That is the symbol for 'om,' which represents the name of god or the vibration of the supreme. It also represents the divine energies of Brahma, Vishnu, and Shiva, which is why they are each shown within the symbol. As you can guess, this is where the hotel gets its name."

"Interesting," the man replied, his expression contemplative. "Anyway, I am here because a friend of mine was supposed to have left a message for me."

"Okay, just a moment," the concierge stated as he tapped on the holographic screen hidden behind the desk. "Can you please give me your name?"

"Gunther Lueschen."

After a moment, the concierge looked up from his screen and smiled. "Yes. I believe I have it here. Can you please confirm the name of the sender?"

"Travis Butler."

"Thank you." Pause. "It appears the sender requested thumbprint confirmation, as well as two security questions. Shall I proceed?"

Hesitating momentarily, the visitor answered in the affirmative.

Nodding, the employee of the hotel tapped the holographic button on his screen and pointed toward the thumb-reading device on the counter. The man carefully placed his left thumb on the reader. A moment later, a green light lit up and a pleasant tone came from the machine.

"Very good," the concierge stated as his guest withdrew his hand from the reader and placed it back at his side. "Here is the first security question: What restaurant did we meet at recently?"

This brought a crease to the hairless brow and his eyes lost their focus for several seconds. Finally, he looked back at the concierge. "Heavenly Helpings."

"Thank you. And the second question: What did I suggest you do at that meeting?"

Again, the man looked contemplative for several seconds before offering the answer. "Visit *Pandora's Box*."

"Excellent," the concierge said with a friendly smile. "Do you have a data reader available, or would you like the message sent in another format?"

"Here." He produced a handheld holographic reader from the pocket of his pinstriped suit coat.

The hotel employee scanned the reader then pressed another button on his screen. "There you go, sir. Will there be anything else I can help you with today?"

The man studied the two-dimensional, private screen for a second, then satisfied that the message was received, he turned his attention back to the other. "No, thank you. You've been most helpful."

"Thank you, sir. We hope to see you again soon at the Om Tower Hotel."

Grabbing the handle of his briefcase, the bald man stepped away from the counter and headed off down the hall of the hotel toward the restaurant and bar section, slipping the reader back into his suit pocket. Upon entering the bar, he sat down on a stool and began chatting politely with one of the bartenders. As he did so, he noticed with interest that the two men whom he had seen earlier while "examining" the decor of the foyer were just entering the area. Both men walked with a confidence and poise that was hard to mistake to a trained eye. In addition, they both had a slight bulge under the left breast of their jackets—exactly where a weapon's holster would be.

These two were not ordinary hotel guests.

Being careful not to be seen observing these new arrivals, the bald man continued conversing casually with the bartender. A moment later, he stood up with his briefcase in his hand and walked toward the back exit, doing his best to look inconspicuous. Unfortunately, his movements did not escape notice. As he feared, his two stalkers moved into action before the exit door closed behind him.

Once through the door, all pretense was forsaken as the casual gait of an apparent businessman was abandoned for the all-out sprint of a hunted fugitive, briefcase clutched to his chest! Using his mental implant, he accessed the schematic of the hotel. The electronic devices connected in his brain brought the images to his mind. As he studied the layout of the building, he heard the door to the restaurant open and one of his pursuers give a shout.

With his heart pounding in his chest, the fugitive decided on his course of action and dove through the door leading into the pool area. Several people milled around the pool and were startled when he burst into the room. Ignoring them, he sprinted into the bathroom and changing rooms. Once inside, he entered one of the stalls and shut the door.

Doing his best to control his breathing, the bald man quickly took off his jacket and turned it inside out. He put it on once again, this time with the inner brown-leather lining facing out. Grabbing the seam of his suit pants, he undid the secret clasps and removed them, revealing the faded pair of blue jeans he was wearing underneath. Finally, he removed his glasses and touched the back of his ear with his index finger. Instantly, the holographic image that had been projecting a bald scalp flicked off, leaving in its place a full head of wavy black hair that belonged to Xavier. Tousling his flattened hair quickly, Raptor's wily associate clicked opened his suitcase and tossed the pants and glasses inside as he heard the voices of the two men grow louder as they stepped into the bathroom. Taking a calming breath, he set the briefcase down on the floor behind the toilet and opened the stall door. Walking over to the sinks, he nodded a greeting to an elderly gentleman who was in the process of combing his hair in the mirror. Just as he began to check his own reflection, his pursuers stepped around the corner.

"Whoa!" Xavier exclaimed in feigned shock at the sight of his burly pursuers. The older man also paused what he was doing and stared in surprise at the newcomers. After a cursory glance in their direction, the two agents ignored them and continued their search for their quarry.

After waiting patiently for several more tense seconds, the con man headed in the opposite direction of the others and exited the changing room back into the hotel. Knowing that his time was limited, he paused just long enough to send a mental message via his implant, then ducked out the nearest hotel exit. Within thirty seconds of leaving the building, the same black hovercar that had dropped him off at the entrance pulled up alongside him. Opening the door, he jumped inside. Even before he had the door closed completely behind him, the driver began heading around the building back toward the main entrance.

"That was a little too close for my taste," Xavier let out a sigh as he sank into the passenger seat.

"So who do you think they were?" Raptor asked as he searched the rearview mirror for any signs of pursuit.

"My best guess would be ESF. They looked like 'em, and they sure followed their protocol."

"But how would Mathison have known to watch the hotel?" Gunther asked from the backseat. Beside him, Jade was peering out the back window with a set of sight-enhancers pressed against her face.

"He's got eyes and ears everywhere," Raptor stated. "When you and Travis disappeared, it wouldn't have been difficult for him to put two and two together. Then, he probably had his people do a thorough search of anything they could find on you or Travis. They would have found the message at the hotel easily. Based on the security measures your friend placed on the message, he's obviously smart enough to figure out that Elysium Security would be after him. Hopefully he's covered his tracks well enough."

"Yeah, speaking of that security, it was a good thing you suggested making a copy of Gunther's thumbprint," Xavier said as he slowly peeled the thin layer of skin-like material off of his left thumb. "And I know I've said it before, but I *really* love these holographic mask projectors," he said emphatically as he removed the pair of small devices from his temples. "They sure beat those old prosthetics and makeup applications. A whole lot less messy too."

"It was fortunate that you both have the implants so that you could relay the security questions back and forth. Thank you for taking this risk on my behalf," Gunther said somberly.

"Ah, don't mention it," Xavier said in mock dismissal. "This was nothing. Remind me to tell you sometime how we pulled off a scam on this Chinese conglomerate. Now *that* was a scam!"

Gunther leaned back, his tone serious. "Again, thank you both. I realize now that I never would have succeeded on my own."

"No kidding," Xavier quipped. "They would've nabbed you before you even made it up to the desk. Welcome to the underworld, old man. You're a wanted man like the rest of us!"

"We're in the clear," Jade said calmly. Removing the sight-enhancers, she placed them in a pouch around her waist and turned around to sit facing forward. "We don't have a tail."

"Great," Raptor said, a hint of relief in his voice. "Now, Xavier, let's find out exactly what the message says."

5

CAUTIOUS RENDEZVOUS

"So according to the message, Gunther's pal, Travis, appears to be hiding out in one of the seedier parts of the *Shudras* level," Raptor said, once they had returned to the clinic. Braedon, whose arm had been treated and bandaged, had now rejoined the group in one of the small, private rooms at the back of the clinic. "Based on the precautions he's already taken to protect the message, he probably received notice the moment Xavier picked it up from the concierge."

"Then he'll be waiting for us," Gunther stated. Eager to be reunited with his friend, the scientist stood to his feet.

"Not so fast, old man," Raptor said, holding up a hand to stop Gunther. "Even though your friend seems to have covered his tracks, we have no idea what to expect. We could be walking into a trap. And if that isn't the case, we don't know whether or not someone followed him to our meeting. Just to make sure, Jade, I want you and Xavier to take the Cliffjumper and follow behind us. Have Zei fly ahead and let me know if you see anything out of the ordinary from his camera implant feeds." Recognizing its name, the little bat-winged mammal on Jade's shoulder chirped noisily as its tiny black eyes stared up at Raptor.

"Braedon, I want you to approach the apartment," Raptor continued. "With your wounded arm and the *svith* scratches on your face, it should hopefully put Travis at ease enough to get him to talk to you. If you notice anything out of place, contact me via implant, and we'll get you out of there. Otherwise, we'll proceed with the meeting. Jade, once Travis is with us, I want you to head over to Durrand's shop. See if you can convince him to trade out the Cliffjumper with something similar, like a Corsair Spelunker. Xavier—"

"If ya don't mind, boss," Xavier said, his face lined with fatigue, "I'd prefer to sit this whole thing out. I need to blow off some steam. All of this 'saving the world' stuff can be quite nerve-racking."

Raptor glanced at the con artist for a moment, his expression hard. Wilting under the scrutiny, Xavier rolled his eyes back in irritation. "What? Are you still gonna hold that against me? C'mon, Raptor. I know I screwed up before and got a little…overzealous for the Box. But I'm clean now."

"Yeah, after nearly getting us killed because you decided to play 'just one more round,'" Jade shot back, her tone accusatory.

"A fact of which I'm *eternally* sorry and promise to never repeat," Xavier stated in a tone of voice of one who had repeated the same phrase numerous times. "But you guys know that I'm the one who really stuck my neck out this time. Cut me a little slack, you rigid bunch of—"

"Fine, Xavier," Raptor said, putting an end to his diatribe. "Once we've picked up Travis, Jade can drop you off before she goes to Durrand's. But before you go getting lost in Pandora's Box, I want to you to contact Fulmala and see if you can get us a temporary place to stay. Don't get carried away this time. I want you back before the sleep cycle. We're sure to have plenty to do tomorrow, and I need you with us."

Pleased that things had gone his way, Xavier sat down on one of the chairs, his expression smug.

"Now, unless anyone *else* has an objection, I suggest we get going."

As Raptor led them out of the room, he locked eyes with Jade. *After you're finished with Durrand's,* he thought, sending the message through the implant, ***take care of that other task we talked about. I want to get that done as soon as possible.***

Understood, she replied, her head nodding slightly in acknowledgment.

―――――――――

Raptor pulled the Obsidian over to the curb about a block away from the meeting place and put the rented hovercar into park, allowing the electric engine to idle noiselessly. Here in the lowest level of the city, named after the *varna* of manual workers, or *Shudras*, poverty was overwhelming. People dressed in rags lined the streets, their emaciated bodies often dirty and unkempt. Filthy children played amongst the garbage that filled the alleys and sidewalks. The majority of the buildings were dilapidated and run down, many with broken windows or no windows at all.

Despite the squalor surrounding him, Raptor was concerned with only one thing. *Jade, what does it look like from above?* Raptor asked through the TC.

Still clear, she replied. *We don't see anything that looks even remotely suspicious.*

Fine. We've circled the area long enough. We're going in, Raptor stated then closed down the link. Turning toward Braedon and Gunther, he relayed the command verbally. "Get ready. Here we go."

Raptor put the Obsidian into gear and moved it into the congested flow of traffic. A minute later, he pulled over once more, this time just a few buildings down from the apartment where Travis would, hopefully, be waiting for them. Without a word, Braedon opened the door of the hovercar. Pulling the cap on his head a little lower to cover his eyes, he stepped out onto the sidewalk and closed the door behind him.

Despite the fact that he'd seen this sad state of humanity multiple times before, he nevertheless found it difficult to focus on the task at hand. Although technology in Tartarus far surpassed that of Earth, Braedon took note of the fact that not all of the residents of this underworld received the benefits of that technology. He bristled at the injustice that people like Mathison and those in the ruling classes in Dehali could live in opulence and splendor, while others less fortunate dwelled in filth and sewage. Steeling himself against his emotions, he walked over to the entrance to the dilapidated apartment complex, leaned toward the voice-activated directory and spoke. "Apartment twenty-seven."

"Thank you," the electronic voice replied. A moment later, a man's voice came through the speaker.

"Yes? What do you want?"

"I'm looking for Travis," Braedon replied. "I'm here on behalf of Gunther Lueschen."

Pause. "Where is he?"

"He's close by. He got your message at the hotel and would like to meet," Braedon said.

"Fine," the voice said. "However, I need proof first that Gunther really is with you."

"Yes, we expected that," Braedon said. "I'm in touch with him through the TC. Ask a question that only he would know, and I'll tell you his answer."

"Okay," came the reply. "Where were we when Gunther first met my wife?"

Braedon relayed the question to Raptor through the implant. A few seconds later, Raptor replied with Gunther's answer. "He says he met her at the Celestial Celebration of Gratitude. He met your wife just before Governor Mathison commenced the Illumination of the Celestial Orbs."

An audible sigh came through the speaker. "Thank the Celestials! Please, come on up!"

"Actually," Braedon said, cutting into the man's enthusiasm, "we would feel more comfortable if you would come with us in our vehicle. We're not certain if this area is secure."

After a brief pause, the man replied. "Sure, as long as I can see Gunther before I get into the vehicle."

"That won't be a problem," Braedon said.

"Okay, I'm coming down."

While he waited, Braedon nonchalantly searched his surroundings for any sign of the ESF. Although he didn't see anything amiss, he was still relieved when the door to the building opened up to reveal a middle-aged man with reddish, curly hair sticking out from under a worn baseball cap who was dressed in a black jacket, plain brown T-shirt, and faded blue jeans.

Recognizing the man from Gunther's description, Braedon held out his right hand. "Travis, it's a pleasure to meet you. I'm Braedon."

Taking the offered hand, Travis shook it, even as his eyes darted nervously over Braedon's shoulder. "Nice to meet you," he said, his eyes finally meeting Braedon's. "Where's Gunther?"

"In the black Obsidian down the block," Braedon said as he began leading Travis toward the vehicle.

As they got within twenty feet of the hovercar, the back passenger door opened, and Gunther climbed out. At the sight of his friend, Travis visibly relaxed. Quickening his pace, he closed the gap between them then enveloped the older man in a warm embrace.

"Gunther, I can't…I can't tell you how relieved I am to see you!" Travis stammered as he pulled back to arm's length.

"As am I to see you," Gunther replied. "We have so much to discuss. But I think it would be safer to do so elsewhere."

"Yes, yes, of course," Travis said, casting another glance at his surroundings. Following Gunther, he climbed into the back of the car. Once they were inside, Braedon closed the back door and got into the front passenger seat. The moment everyone was safely inside, Raptor piloted the hovercar quickly down the street. Several minutes later, the car passed the outskirts of the *Shudras* section of the city, leaving behind them the squalor and hopeless humanity.

6

THE TEMPLE

An abandoned Buddhist temple? That's the best Fulmala could do? Raptor stated.

She said it would probably be better suited to our needs than anything else she could come up with, Xavier replied through the implant TC. *Do you want it, or should I ask her to find something else?*

No, we'll take it. Send me the address. Although Raptor wasn't initially very thrilled with the idea, the more he thought about it, the more it began to grow on him. The temple was in the second level, or *Vaishyas* level, named after the *varna* of merchants and farmers. According to Xavier, it was in a fairly secluded area, and the ESF would be less likely to expect their group to be staying in a temple. It also had an added benefit in that the main area of the temple ought to be more than adequate for Gunther and Travis to use as a workshop. And based on the conversation coming from the back seat of the Obsidian, this operation was going to need more space than originally expected.

Then again, that seemed to always be the case. Things were always more expensive and took longer than originally planned. Only in this case, Raptor couldn't afford things to take too long.

Although all the recent activity had succeeded for a time in taking his mind off the prophecy given by Steven, being surrounded by so many temples, idols, and religious symbols made it impossible for him to elude the thoughts of his own mortality for long.

And now, it appeared he was going to be making a religious building his home. But hopefully not for long. Steven's prophecy had given him thirty-one days to live, and it took them seven just to get to Dehali. With most of today already gone, that only left him with twenty-three days. He sure hoped his two passengers could work quickly.

Shaking off his disturbing thoughts, Raptor busied himself with locating their new residence. He'd been driving around the city for the better part of the hour, and despite his misgivings about setting up shop in a temple, he still found himself glad to arrive at the place. Living a life of crime and shady dealings had meant having to be frequently on the run. As such, he had gotten accustomed to having to move into and out of new places. Usually he enjoyed the variety, and he often drew a sense of satisfaction once the location was established. However, under the current circumstances, he doubted he would find the job very rewarding.

"We're here," Raptor said as he pulled into the darkened alley that led to the back entrance of the building. In the fading light coming from the shimmering veins in the cavern ceiling, the group could see that the entire building was about three stories tall and had as many roofs, one stacked upon the other with each successive layer being slightly smaller than the previous one. The topmost portion of the roof came to a sharp peak at the center, while the edges of the bottom layer contained overhangs that extended six feet beyond the side of the building. Although the structure was currently in poor condition, the beauty that remained left no doubt that those who had constructed it did so with precision and care.

"A Buddhist temple?" Travis exclaimed in surprise. "This is where you guys are staying?" he asked, throwing a questioning glance at Gunther.

"I guess so," the older man responded. "This is news to me."

"It meets our needs," Raptor commented dryly. "Once I've opened up the building and made sure everything is clear, you two can bring the weapon inside and start figuring out what we need to do to get it to reverse the portals. No offense, but I'd really like to be done with this little partnership of ours and get my life back on track."

"Believe me, we agree completely," Gunther stated. "You can rest assured we'll be working as fast as we can. Travis and I would like nothing more than to get back to our families and return to our lives as well."

"Good," Raptor said matter-of-factly. "It's nice to know we're all on the same page." Without another word, he opened the car door and walked toward the back entrance of the temple. Braedon, Gunther, and Travis had been waiting for nearly five minutes before Braedon received the TC message from Raptor via that it was safe. After retrieving the satchel that contained the Vortex weapon from the trunk of the car, the three men went inside.

As expected for a run-down, abandoned building, the interior was full of dust and small debris. The door that the three men entered through led them into a hallway. Based on what little they could see in the darkness, it appeared that this area consisted of smaller rooms, probably dedicated to either offices or small prayer rooms and bathrooms. Continuing on down the hallway, they followed the instructions transmitted from Raptor until they reached a door at the far end.

Opening the door, they were momentarily blinded as they stepped into the brightly lit room. The rectangular central chamber was one hundred twenty feet wide and twice that in length. Taking up much of the room were several rows of what appeared to be small cushions. Each cushion was three-foot square and rested upon a short base about six inches high. The layout was set up so that there were eight rows consisting of twelve individual cushions on both sides of a wide, central aisle, as well as spacious side aisles between the end of the rows and the walls.

Although now covered with dust and somewhat yellowed from disuse, the walls and ceiling were covered in beautiful patterns of reds, golds, and blues. At the far end, surrounded by exquisitely carved swirls of gold that outlined the form of the statue, was an enormous Buddha sitting in the traditional lotus position, with its legs crossed beneath it.

A loud sneeze suddenly interrupted the silence. Turning around, Braedon looked over at Travis, who was wiping his nose with a handkerchief. "Sorry," he said apologetically. "It's the dust."

"Well, you're going to have to get used to it," Raptor said as he entered the room from the wide double doors at the opposite end of the room from the statue. "At least until we get this place cleaned up. My acquaintance recently discovered this building, and one of her stipulations on us staying here was that we fix it up a little so she can use it later."

"If there *is* a later," Travis commented. "Based on what Gunther told me in the car, things aren't looking too good right now."

"Which is all the more reason for the two of you to get to work," Raptor retorted snidely. "Braedon and I will clear these cushions off to the sides of the room and get rid of this dust. Let me know as soon as possible what it is we need to do to get this thing to work."

Gunther exchanged a concerned glance with his partner before returning his attention to Raptor. "You do understand, of course, that this is going to take a while. We have tons of data to sift through before we even get a grasp on what kinds of alterations the developers of the Vortex weapon did with my original Portal Stabilizer design. Then, we'll need to get the parts and—"

"Yes, I know," Raptor interrupted in irritation. "You've explained all this to me before. Just get started." He began to turn away from the two scientists but then reversed direction. "Oh, and one more thing, we don't want anyone knowing we're here. So until we get some black spray on the windows, don't turn on any lights in any rooms with windows. I'll put some tape over the switches as a reminder until we get something more permanent in place."

They all set about their various tasks. Braedon and Raptor both worked in silence as they cleaned up the main room, while Gunther and Travis sat down on a couple of cushions and began sorting through the data that Gunther had downloaded from the Elysium government building.

After more than two hours, Braedon had finished cleaning most of the central room. With his left arm still bandaged, the work had been tougher than normal. Sitting down on one of the cushions, he relaxed and began to study the giant Buddha statue while the two scientists continued to discuss the intricacies of wormholes and portals. Lost in thought, he didn't notice Raptor until the man was standing within arm's length.

"Have you ever been in a temple before?" Raptor asked.

"No, I haven't."

"How does it feel to be in a building devoted to a 'false' religion? Do you feel some kind of...demonic presence?" Raptor goaded.

Braedon thought for a moment before responding. "Honestly, I do feel something, but I wouldn't say it's a 'demonic presence.' I mostly feel a sense of...sadness."

"Sadness?" Raptor repeated in surprise. "Why sadness?"

"Do you remember our conversation just after Steven's death?"

"Of course."

"Then you understand that from my perspective, the people who came to worship in this place were completely lost and misguided," Braedon said.

Raptor scoffed. "Spoken like a true religious zealot. I suppose you feel the same way about all of the Hindus in this city as well. Look, I know we talked about this whole 'absolute truth' thing, but don't you think it's a bit presumptuous to believe that you have a corner on the truth? Isn't it prideful and snobbish to think that you're right and everyone else is wrong?"

Braedon stood up and walked over to stand in front of the statue of Buddha. After a moment, he turned back around to face Raptor. "What would you say if I told you that I believe that a herd of *griblins* spoke to me and told me that Celestials want all of us to paint our hair pink to show our love for them?"

Despite his general dislike of the Christian and his beliefs, Raptor still laughed at the absurd question. "I'd say that the people who installed your implant got a few wires crossed!"

"Exactly," Braedon replied, a grin of his own creeping its way onto his face. "So you do recognize that not all beliefs should be given the same weight, right?"

"Okay, sure," Raptor said in acquiescence.

"Well, I'm convinced, based on logic and the evidence I've seen, that Christianity is true," Braedon stated. "If you disagree with me, then prove me wrong. You present your case, and I'll present mine. If you want to do that, I'd be more than happy to oblige. But," he said snidely, "if you want to be like the majority of our modern society and take the easy way out by hurling insults at me and calling me a religious bigot instead of thinking through the evidence logically, that's up to you."

Raptor's first impulse was to punch the man in the face, and at just about any other time in his life, he would have done that. Then again, if he did so, he would only prove Braedon's point. *Fine, I'll play his game. His religion is* full *of logical holes. If I give him enough rope, he'll hang himself,* Raptor thought inwardly. *That is, unless he really does have good answers. What will you do then?* The unwelcome thought intruded itself into his mind. Casting it aside, he turned his focus back to the conversation.

"Okay. Then tell me why you don't believe Buddhism is correct," Raptor challenged as he sat down on a pair of nearby cushions and reclined onto one elbow.

Accepting the invitation to verbally spar, Braedon began pacing as he considered how best to phrase his answer. "What do you know about the basic beliefs of Buddhism?"

Raptor shrugged. "I don't know. They believe in reincarnation and following a bunch of rules so that you can get rid of bad karma and achieve nirvana. They also believe in meditation and worshipping a guy named Buddha."

"Okay, so you've got some of it right," Braedon said. "Although many Buddhists don't worship Buddha at all. As with nearly all religions, there are some variations in the doctrines. I'll try to stick to the core beliefs. Basically, Buddhism is more of a moral philosophy than a religion. It teaches that life is full of suffering, we suffer because we crave things, so in order to stop suffering, we need to stop craving." Turning around, Braedon walked over to the Buddha statue and pointed to some small writing that was carved into the wall. "The way to do that is through meditation and by following the Noble Eightfold Path."

Curious, Raptor got up from the cushion and walked over to inspect the writing, which was in both English and Hindi. As he did so, Braedon began to read off the titles of each one. "Right Understanding, Right Thought, Right Speech, Right Action, Right Livelihood, Right Effort, Right Mindfulness, and Right Concentration. In addition to this, there are the Five Precepts that Buddhists follow, which form the basis of their morality."

"Just what I said," Raptor stated in disgust, "they have to follow a bunch of rules."

"And these rules," Braedon said, "if followed, should help them break out of the cycle of reincarnation in order to achieve Nirvana, which basically means that you as a person enter a permanent state of nonexistence. Unlike the

Christian or Islamic understanding of a paradise where the soul lives forever, the goal of Buddhism is to disappear like a drop of water in the ocean."

Raptor scoffed. "That sounds like fun. Where do I sign up?"

Braedon smiled as he turned away from the statue and the writing to face his companion. "Exactly. Now, if you go back to our previous conversation, you'll remember that I mentioned that each religion must answer four basic questions, right?"

"Yeah," Raptor said flippantly.

"Okay, so let me use those questions to summarize the beliefs of Buddhism then.

"One: Where did we come from? What's the origin of the universe and of life?" Braedon asked as he held up one finger to count off his points. "Buddhism doesn't have a definitive answer on this. To the Buddhist, this question is irrelevant. The focus of Buddhism is to liberate oneself from suffering in the *present*, not the past or the future."

Raising his middle finger to join the first, Braedon continued. "Two: Why is there pain and suffering? As I mentioned a moment ago, Buddhists believe that we suffer because we crave things. The whole issue of suffering is what their Four Noble truths are all about. However, as far as I know, Buddhists don't attempt to answer the question of where pain and suffering originated from.

"Three: What is the meaning of life?" Braedon asked, pointing to his third finger. "Buddha taught that the only real purpose of life is to end suffering. This is why many serious Buddhists forego marriage," Braedon stated with a grin.

Raptor couldn't help himself and laughed out loud, causing Gunther and Travis to momentarily pause in their work on the other side of the room. As his mirth subsided, Raptor looked down at Braedon's left hand and noticed for the first time that the soldier wore a wedding ring. He opened his mouth to make a comment about it when Braedon, seeing the focus of the man's gaze, cut him off.

"Finally: What's going to happen to us when we die?" Braedon asked, his fourth finger rising to join the other three. "Again, as we already mentioned, the goal is to end the cycle of reincarnation and cease to exist.

"Now, one of the things I told you that is most important about determining truth in a court case is asking the questions: 'Who says?' and 'By what authority?'" Braedon said. "If a Buddhist is going to convince you that all this stuff is true, then he has to convince you that Buddha himself knew what he was talking about. What do you know about the origin of Buddhism?"

"I don't know," Raptor replied. "I had a hard enough time learning the history of Tartarus in school, much less learning about Earth history and religious people. It was never important."

"Well, if you hope to build a case for *your* beliefs, it's pretty important to question the authority of *other* belief systems, don't you think?" Braedon retorted. "The original Buddha was a man by the name of Siddhartha Gautama who was an Indian prince around the fifth century BC. He lived a life full of wealth and pleasure until one day he went on a journey and saw an old man, a sick man, and a corpse. It hit him that nothing lasted in this life. Everything passes away, which is the cause for suffering."

"That sounds about right," Raptor said derisively.

Ignoring the comment, Braedon continued. "He was so impacted by this that he left his wife and infant son and went on a search for truth and meaning. After six years, he sat beneath a tree and promised himself that he wouldn't move until he attained 'enlightenment.' He sat there for many days until he finally felt that he had become an 'Enlightened One,' which is what *Buddha* means. He spent the rest of his life teaching others how to find this 'path' to freedom from suffering.

"Now, with all of that background, let me ask you this," Braedon said, his eyes burning into Raptor's, "what evidence do we have that anything that Buddha taught is true?"

Raptor was silent for a moment as he pondered Braedon's question. "Well, there have been many people who believe they can remember past lives."

"Yeah, but how do you know that *they* are telling the truth?" Braedon countered. "Besides, there's a logical problem with the whole idea of reincarnation to begin with. According to Buddhism, there's no God who created everything. Therefore, who's in charge of reincarnation? Who set that 'law' in place? Who's 'keeping score' regarding karma? You can't have a law without a lawgiver."

"Hmm, good point," Raptor stated. "So if what you're saying is true and not just some version of Buddhism that you Christians make up in order to make it easy to tear down, anyone who believes in Buddhism is putting their faith in the teachings of a single man who is supposedly 'enlightened.'"

Braedon nodded. "Pretty much."

Frowning, Raptor took a step closer to Braedon, as if to challenge him. "Then tell me, why do you believe that

Christianity is any different? Aren't you just following the teachings of one man also?"

Without hesitating, Braedon stood his ground and replied confidently, "Yes and no. Jesus is central to Christianity, but the Bible is much more than just a collection of his teachings. It's filled with historical facts and eyewitness accounts that span the entire history of the Earth, from its creation until about sixty years after the death and resurrection of Jesus. It isn't just one book, but rather a *library* of sixty-six books written by over forty authors in three different languages over a span of four thousand years!"

Braedon paused to gauge how his words were impacting the other man. To his surprise, Raptor remained stoic yet attentive. Encouraged, Braedon continued. "So if you were standing in a courtroom and judging a case, whom would you be more inclined to believe? Would you believe the testimony of one witness, or that of over forty witnesses?"

Before Raptor could respond to the question, Gunther's voice suddenly rose in pitch as he called out to Raptor and Braedon from the other side of the room. "We found it!"

"What?" Raptor asked, all thoughts of his conversation with Braedon abandoned. Turning toward the two scientists, he strode over to where they stood examining the data. "What have you found?"

Smiling in triumph, Gunther pointed to the holographic display screen. "It turns out they didn't make nearly as many changes as we thought! We were able to identify the main alterations they made in our original design. We can do this! With just a little more research, we're confident we'll be able to stabilize the portals!"

7

DARK AND LIGHT

*Darkness…cold stone beneath his fingertips…a distant light…
a low growl behind him…*

Raptor recognized these surroundings. They had been haunting him now for weeks.

He was having the nightmare again.

The growl grew in intensity behind him, causing him to glance in that direction. Intense, mind-numbing fear washed over him. Without conscious thought, Raptor ran toward the light.

"Stop!" he screamed inwardly. "This isn't real!"

Despite his frantic efforts to regain control of his own body and emotions, he felt himself being inexorably drawn down the tunnel until it opened into the familiar chamber. In the center of the enormous room, shining brightly as it always did, was the beautiful, jewel-encrusted sword, the blade of which was stuck halfway into the granite pedestal.

"NO!" Raptor yelled. He knew what was about to happen…what had happened every single time he experienced this nightmare.

The creature was coming for him…

Lurching forward, he struggled toward the sword. However, though he strained with every ounce of his waning strength, the pure radiance that shone forth from the weapon sent him crashing to his knees. Behind him, he could sense the presence of the mighty beast as it entered the chamber. Unable to resist, he glanced over his shoulder to see the massive batlike wings unfurl and hover over its lithe, serpentine body. Although the light from the sword filled the chamber, the black scales of the creature seemed to somehow deflect the light rather than absorb it, making it appear as nothing more than a shimmering shadow.

The creature's forked tongue moved rapidly across its razor-like teeth as its reptilian head drew closer to him. "You are mine, Rahib Ahmed," the low, guttural voice dripped from the beast's mouth. It spoke his name slowly, as if relishing each syllable.

Paralyzed by fear, he suddenly felt a burning rage tear through his soul. "Why can't I use the sword? Why is it even here if I can't use it!"

Behind him, the serpent laughed, the throaty, evil sound sending a chill through Raptor's heart, freezing his very soul. Crushed, Raptor cried out in frustration and anguish one last time then collapsed onto the cold, stone floor of the chamber, the beast's laughter echoing around him…

Raptor awakened with a jolt and instantly sat up in his makeshift bed, his heart racing. Although he and the others had been living in the temple already for two days, his dazed mind was confused by his surroundings, causing a panic to grip him momentarily. Then, as he returned to full consciousness, he gradually forced his way through the cloudy fog of the receding nightmare. He remembered that he had fallen asleep on an old couch in one of the side rooms of the Buddhist temple. Finally, after several long moments, he felt the tension fade away, leaving him feeling empty and drained.

Although he fought to keep from dwelling on the nightmare, he couldn't help but wonder at its meaning. Steven said it was given to him as a sign from God. *How is it possible to respect someone and think they're crazy at the same time?* Raptor wondered. *How could Steven have been so intelligent, yet believe so much nonsense?* Reaching into his jacket pocket, he removed his holographic reader that contained Steven's journal. Raptor hated religion. Why then did he find Steven's ramblings so intriguing?

Despite the inner voice that seemed to laugh at him for wasting his time reading such foolishness, Raptor turned on the device and read the next entry.

One of the most foundational questions that everyone must wrestle with is the question of whether or not there is a God. Before you can consider which religion is the truth, you have to first consider if there is any reason to believe in a creator at all! If the answer is "no," then all religions are false. Is there evidence that we were created, or did the entire universe just come about by random chance? This question can actually be answered with two simple, logical arguments.

1. *Information can only be created by intelligence.*
2. *Something cannot come from nothing.*

Let's consider the first point. Have you ever thought about information before? Information has no extra matter! A blank data disc and a full data disc contain the same amount of matter. The only difference is that the full data disc contains matter that is arranged in a particular fashion that, when read by someone who understands the code, relays a message. For exam-

ple, this very journal you are reading contains words written in English in a particular order to create a message. If the words were jumbled, or if the words were written in a language that you didn't understand, such as Spanish, then the message wouldn't make sense.

What does this have to do with God? Well, the same principle applies to life. All life contains messages written in the code of DNA. There is enough DNA information in one human to fill one thousand books of five hundred pages each! Since scientists have never observed a single instance where a code system came about from natural causes, it is only logical that our DNA must have been created by an intelligence.

Aha! But those who believe in the Celestials would argue that aliens could be the creators! However, this doesn't truly solve the problem. All it does is push the issue back further. If the Celestials created us, then who created them? Did they evolve? If we are so complex that our existence demands a creator, then any beings that created us would have to be even more intelligent and require and even more intelligent creator. And on and on you go.

Point number two. In order for evolution to work, you have to take it back farther and farther in time. How did life evolve? Well, that depends on how the Earth evolved. How did the Earth evolve? Well, that depends on how the universe evolved. Eventually, you get back to the beginning of the universe. According to evolutionary scientists, the universe began as a "singularity," which is a dot the size of a period that supposedly contained all of the matter in the entire universe. This dot then exploded to create the universe. But where did the singularity come from? Science has never observed a single instance where nothing created something, much less an explosion that resulted in complexity. Just the opposite is true.

But then, if there is a God, who created him? The short answer is: no one. He has always existed. This makes sense logically because God created time itself! God is outside of time.

Ultimately, if you want to disregard observable science and believe that information and a code system can be created randomly, and that nothing can create something, that's up to you. But to say that belief in God is unscientific is purely wrong.

Furthermore—

Suddenly, the slight, tingling sensation and soft beep that always indicated an incoming implant call interrupted his reading. Shutting off the holographic reader, he stood up and focused his attention on the voice coming through the Telekinetic Connection.

Raptor, it's Janak.

What's the word on Charon? Raptor asked, his current mood leaving no patience for courtesies.

He's conscious, and in a foul mood, Janak said.

If he hadn't just awoken from a horrendous nightmare a few minutes ago, Raptor would have smiled at the thought. Instead, he simply settled for sarcasm. ***When is he not in a foul mood?***

Unamused, Janak continued his report. ***Anyway, I'm sure he'll be TC you as soon as the nurse is finished changing his bandages. He wants to leave, and at this point, I...I think that would be best.***

Raptor frowned, not liking the direction this conversation was heading. ***What's that supposed to mean?***

It means that, in addition to Charon's serious attitude problem, I...I think it would be best if you... Look, don't take this wrong. We've always helped each other out, but this time... It's just...I just found out that the ESF has sent a whole team of Guardians to Dehali to find you!

8

PLANS

Raptor closed his eyes and sighed heavily, his fears verified. *A whole team, huh? Are they in Dehali yet?* Raptor replied.

From what I heard, they were originally scattered out, searching the Fringe areas closest to Elysium trying to find you. However, something must have happened, because they were last seen heading straight for Dehali. They'll probably be here in about three days **if** *they wait to regroup. If not, some of them could be here sooner. So,* Janak paused, *I think it's best if you pick up Charon and don't come back for a long time. I don't know what trouble you've gotten into, but I don't want any part of it.*

Raptor swore out loud in frustration before returning to the implant conversation. *Fine. I'll be by in an hour.* Closing down the link, Raptor grabbed his jacket and headed out the door to find the others. *Xavier, Jade, Braedon, meet me in the workshop,* he commanded in a group TC.

As he entered the central room of the temple, Gunther stood up from where he and Travis were working and walked forward to greet him. "I know it's taken us almost two full days, but we're pretty sure we've finished the list,"

Gunther stated, his voice filled with excitement. "If we can get a hold of these tools and parts, we should be able to…" His words trailed off as he noticed the dark expression on Raptor's face. "What is it? What's wrong?"

"I'll tell you in a moment," Raptor stated. "Let me see the list."

Gunther numbly handed the man his holographic data reader, concern about Raptor's negative demeanor causing his previous excitement to drain away. As Raptor began studying the list, the far door opened up, and Jade and Xavier entered the room. Engrossed in the information just handed to him, Raptor held up a hand to indicate that the two newcomers were not to interrupt him. A few moments later, he turned his attention back to the two scientists.

"Are you sure this is all you need?" he asked.

Gunther glanced at Travis before nodding. "As much as possible. There are always variables that are impossible to predict, but we think this will suffice."

"What's going on?" Xavier asked curiously as Braedon entered the room through the main double doors.

With everyone assembled, Raptor addressed them. "There's been a new development. Janak just informed me that a team of Guardians are on their way to Dehali to find us."

"What?" Travis exclaimed as he exchanged a worried glance with Gunther.

"It seems that after we disappeared from Elysium, the ESF sent out the Guardians to scour the Fringe for us," Raptor said. "It probably took them a couple of days to find out that Travis had left a note for Gunther at the hotel. Knowing they couldn't get to Dehali ahead of us, they contacted their agents already in the city to watch the hotel.

Once Xavier picked up the message, they knew we were here. At that point, they regrouped the Guardians and sent them after us."

"So…so what do we do now?" Gunther asked, fear causing his voice to tremble.

"We stick to the plan, only now we have to be a little more careful with our movements," Raptor replied.

"What exactly is the plan?" Braedon asked.

Looking around at each of them in turn, Raptor began outlining their next moves. "Gunther and Travis have compiled a list of materials they're going to need to convert the Vortex weapon back into the Portal Stabilizer," he said as he passed the holo reader to Jade. Xavier and Braedon moved closer to her, and the three of them read through the information as Raptor continued. "The list isn't long, but some of the items are hard to come by. So we're going to contact Sarbjeet. He should be able to get us what we need."

"I don't recognize all of these items, but I do know that magnetic transducers don't come cheap," Braedon stated. "Were you planning on purchasing them, or acquire them through 'other' means?"

"How Sarbjeet gets them isn't the point," Raptor retorted. "One way or the other, we *are* going to have to pay him for getting them for us, which brings up another issue. So far, my team has had to foot the bill for this little operation. I think it's time for the rest of you to 'donate' to the cause."

Travis looked at Gunther once more, his expression downcast. "I don't have anything to offer. My family and I left everything we had in Elysium. We've been scraping by in one of the poorest sections of the city. I withdrew all of my credits from the bank before leaving Elysium, but my family needs those credits to keep us going until I find a better job."

Gunther grimaced. "I have credits in the bank, but it… the ESF are bound to have placed tracers on my accounts. If I withdraw any credits now, they'll find us for sure."

Expecting Raptor to be angry, Gunther was surprised to see that he merely appeared thoughtful. After a short visual exchange with Jade, Raptor turned his attention to Braedon. "Well, what's your excuse?" he said sarcastically.

Braedon met the man's gaze firmly. "My decision to help Gunther wasn't premeditated. So all of my credits are in the bank as well. However, I may have a way to get some."

Raptor raised one eyebrow. Then, as realization struck him, he nodded in understanding. "Right. Your Crimson Liberty friends. Am I to assume, then, that they have a cell here in Dehali as well?"

"Yes," Braedon confirmed. "I'll get in contact with them. They may not be able to offer much, but it should help."

"Good," Raptor said. "I'm also going to need you and Gunther to give me access information for you bank accounts."

Confusion passed over Gunther's features. "But…what good will that do? The tracers…"

Raptor cut him off. "Don't worry about it. I know what I'm doing. I just want you to focus on getting that thing to work."

Looking over at the Vortex weapon sitting on its tripod, Gunther cleared his throat. "Um…there's one more thing we need to discuss."

"And that is?" Raptor asked with a frown.

"In order to calibrate the machine properly, we need to do an analysis of one of the portals while it is open."

Silence hung in the air for several moments as they each processed the statement. Finally, Xavier spoke, his inflection one of incredulity. "Are you crazy? Do you think the government of Dehali is just going to let you walk up to their portal and say, 'Hey, guys! Don't mind me. I'm just taking a few readings'? Maybe you ignorant, average citizens believe that politicians don't divulge information to each other, but in our line of work, we've seen firsthand how Mathison and Governor Khatri work together. You've got to assume that anything that Khatri's people see, Mathison sees."

"Yes, I know that," Gunther said in frustration. "But there's no other way. We *have* to get that data! These portals transcend time and space! We can't duplicate that effect randomly! We *have* to base our calculations on the original portals."

"Can we relocate to another city and use their portal to get the readings?" Jade asked.

Gunther shrugged. "Perhaps. Travis and I *did* discuss that option. But where else can we go? Elysium and Dehali are out, so that leaves only Bab al-Jihad, New China, the European States, and the United African Nations."

"No," Raptor stated sharply. "We do it here. Bab al-Jihad is not an option, and the other three are all the way on the other side of the Well. It would take us too long to get there, and the situation would remain the same regardless. Although the governors of New China, the Euro States, and UAN are not overly fond of Mathison, I don't think they'd hesitate to turn us over to him in order to win political points. We'll just have to make it work."

"How?" Xavier asked, clearly not happy with the direction the conversation had taken.

"We'll come up with something," Raptor replied. "For now, we have work to do. Travis and Gunther, keep doing what you can until we can get you these items."

"I'd also like to go home for a little while," Travis interrupted. "I haven't seen my family for days."

"I don't think that's wise at this point," Raptor said. "We need to keep our movements to a minimum. *Especially* you and Gunther. We'll pick up your family and bring them here. That way, you won't have to worry about their safety and can focus on your work. Besides, it would be helpful to have someone here to take care of food preparation and cleaning. That is, as long as your children won't get in our way."

Travis looked relieved. "No. Cage is fourteen and Marissa is twelve. They can help Sandy cook and clean."

"Good," Raptor said. "After we're finished here, contact your wife and let her know to be ready. Now, the first thing we need to do is pick up Charon from Janak's medical center. Xavier, you drive the new Spelunker Jade got from Durrand. You and Charon will provide backup if necessary."

"Don't you mean *I'll* provide backup," Xavier quipped. "With all the pain meds they've probably given him, Charon's likely to be less help than my granny after she's drank too much *juri-juice.*"

"I wouldn't be so sure," Raptor stated with a grin. "He's already contacted me once via implant since we've been talking, and if his ranting is any indicator, he's quite coherent."

"Oh, great. That's even better," Xavier mumbled under his breath. "I get to sit inside a van with a wounded, angry Charon! I think I'd prefer to be thrown into a cage with a hungry *tunrokla.*"

Ignoring Xavier's quiet tirade, Raptor refocused the conversation. "Jade, I want you and Braedon to come with me. We'll take the Obsidian and see if Sarbjeet can help us. Although we've worked together in the past, I don't completely trust him. Be ready for anything. Braedon, how's your arm?"

"I can use it if necessary," Braedon stated. "The wounds were deep, but the arm's not broken. However, I think I'll leave the sling on for now but loosen the straps so I can take it off quickly in an emergency."

"Good idea. After we get the items we need and are sure that everything is clear, Xavier, I want you and Charon to pick up Travis's wife and children in the Spelunker and bring them back here. Braedon, once we've returned, I want you to meet with your friends so that we can get Sarbjeet paid off. I don't want to give him a reason to turn on us. Any questions?"

"Yes," Xavier spoke up. "What's for lunch?"

Raptor smirked. "We're not stopping on the way, if that's what you're asking. Just grab something from the supplies that you and Jade bought. Now let's get moving. We leave in five minutes!"

9

CONNECTIONS

"It's about time! When are you getting me out of here? The food tastes worse than *igri* slop!"

Laughing, Raptor strode over to where Charon lay on one of the medical center's thin mats, which appeared particularly small when compared to the man's large, muscular frame. He was dressed in loose-fitting pants, with his bare chest and arms covered only in bandages in various places. "It's nice to see you too, Caleb," Raptor said sarcastically. "Actually, it turns out the employees here love your 'charming personality' so much, they were hoping you'd become a permanent addition to their staff."

Charon frowned and threw an irritated look in Raptor's direction. "Yeah, that's real funny," he said, his voice oozing with sarcasm of his own. "What's been goin' on? I want outta here."

Raptor grabbed a folding chair that had been leaning against the wall and set it up near Charon's mat. Turning it around, Raptor straddled the chair, his arms leaning on the back support. "Well, I saved your life, for one thing," he began. "That *svith* nearly took you out. Maybe if you weren't such a wimp, I wouldn't have to always save your skin."

Charon grinned, his mood lightening. "Yeah right."

"Anyway, we brought you here to get patched up, contacted Gunther's buddy, and moved in to an abandoned Buddhist temple," Raptor continued. "That was two days ago. The old man and his sidekick have been hard at work ever since. They just completed a list of stuff they're going to need, and we're on our way to meet with Sarbjeet to see if he can help us out. Are you interested in tagging along? That is, if you aren't too weak to—"

"Shut up and get out of my way," Charon said as he rose unsteadily to his feet. Laughing again, Raptor tossed his friend his regular clothes so he could change. Once Charon was ready, the two of them met with Janak briefly, paid him, and headed out of the clinic.

"I need you to ride with Xavier in the Spelunker," Raptor said as he and Charon approached the vehicles. As his friend opened up his mouth to protest, Raptor quickly cut him off. "If you were fully recovered, I'd want you by my side in a second. But until then, I need your eyes alert for trouble. I'll TC you and fill you in on the plan along the way."

"Fine. But only this once," Charon said irritably. "Just because I'm full of cuts and scrapes doesn't mean I can't hold my own."

"C'mon," Raptor said as he cast a cursory glance at their surroundings. "We need to get moving." The moment they were both settled in the vehicles, the Obsidian and Spelunker pulled away from the clinic and headed toward the bridge that would take them to the third level of the city.

"Your friend must have some pretty powerful connections," Braedon stated in admiration as Jade drove the Obsidian through the main gate and down the private driveway toward the mansion.

Sarbjeet's residence was located in the third tier of the city called the *Kshatriyas*, which was reserved for the ruling class of governors, politicians, and military personnel. Unlike the *Shudras* level, the buildings and streets in this section were well-maintained and immaculate. Based on the size of Sarbjeet's mansion and the level of artistry evident on the fascia and pillars framing the main entrance, Braedon knew that he was about to meet a man of considerable power and influence.

"Based on the apparent *lack* of security, I'd guess he's got numerous camouflage nets in place," Braedon stated as the car drew closer to the building. "How well do you know this guy?"

"We've worked together numerous times," Raptor stated. "I'm sure that Steven mentioned that, for a while, my team had done some odd jobs for Mathison, gathering materials and stuff for his pet projects."

At the mention of his recently deceased mentor's name, Braedon felt a wave of emotional pain pass through him. "Yeah, he told me."

"Well, Sarbjeet was one of my main connections. He's retired Dehali military, so he has connections everywhere. He can get things that no one else can."

"But how can you trust him knowing that he's got ties to Mathison?" Braedon asked, his concern about their current situation rising.

"Because I've seen him turn down Mathison on multiple occasions," Raptor stated. "Sarbjeet has no loyalties.

Even the Dehali Military Corp see him as a loose cannon. As long as we pay him well, we shouldn't have anything to worry about. Besides," he said flippantly, "he owes me."

Sensing that further probing would be pointless, Braedon changed subjects. "So why did we come all the way here? Why didn't you just TC him and let him know what we need? Why are we going through all this trouble?"

"Because that's not the way he works," Raptor said. "Whenever he does any kind of negotiating, he wants it done on *his* turf and in person. It puts the buyer off balance and helps ensure that Sarbjeet gets the best deal possible. It's kind of difficult to tell your host that you don't agree with the terms knowing that you've got multiple, computer-controlled lasers pointed at your head."

"I can imagine," Braedon said dispassionately.

The conversation ended abruptly as Jade brought the vehicle to a stop in front of the main entrance. *Xavier, Charon, are you in position?* Raptor asked over the implant connection.

Yeah, we're here, although I'm not sure exactly how we're going to be any help if you need us. That place is a fortress, Xavier replied.

For one thing, I want you to make sure we didn't have a tail, Raptor responded. *I don't think Sarbjeet would be too happy if we brought a team of ESF agents snooping around. Just stay alert.*

Shutting down the connection, Raptor turned to look at Braedon. "Listen, Sarbjeet can be a little…unpredictable. No matter what happens, TC me first before doing or saying anything. Got it?"

"Yeah," Braedon replied, his vocal inflection and facial expression leaving no doubt that he wasn't happy with Raptor's instructions.

"All right, let's go," Raptor said as he opened the door and exited the vehicle. Putting aside his reservations, Braedon followed the other's lead. When Jade had joined them at the bottom of the steps leading to the mansion's entrance, the Obsidian headed off toward the garages, piloting remotely by the mansion's computer. Two SK-290, heavily armed sentry droids, stood on each side of the stairway, their torsos pivoting to track the trio's movements as they ascended the steps.

The droids had human-shaped torsos and arms, and their heads, while human-sized, lacked any features except a rectangular, sleek sensor bar. Located where the eyes should be, the bar glowed with a dark blue light. Letting his gaze drop down to the arms, Braedon guessed, based on their thickness, that they housed numerous weapons underneath the blue-black color scheme of the armored plating. While the upper body of the automaton was bulky and impressive, the bottom portion was nearly nonexistent. He had seen this design on several occasions and knew that the droid maneuvered by using the same hover technology that were used on other vehicles. Although they now rested on the ground, he knew that, once activated, they would be able to glide effortlessly over any terrain, making them extremely quick and agile.

Upon reaching the top landing, the double doors leading into the mansion slid open to reveal a beautiful young woman dressed in an elegant, sleeveless gown. The triangular designs of gold that were woven into the blue fabric of the gown were matched by a blue scarf with gold trim that was draped loosely over the woman's arms. Accentuating her beauty was a thin strand of diamonds set in gold that rested on the crown of her head and draped down over her forehead between the parts of her braided black hair. Just below the tip of the jewelry, set on her forehead between the eyebrows was a single, red dot. However, despite her dazzling finery and warm smile, Braedon could see hopelessness in her eyes and demeanor.

"Greetings," she said, her eyes lifting only briefly before returning to stare at the floor. "My name is Lajvati. Master Saini is expecting you. Please follow me."

Raptor, Jade, and Braedon followed Lajvati into the mansion. As they strode into the foyer, Braedon couldn't help but be impressed with the luxurious surroundings. Tapestries, paintings, plants, and pottery of various designs and artistry lined the walls, many of which framed or drew attention to the hundreds of small statues of the various gods and goddesses of the Hindu religion that filled the hallway.

This friend of yours seems to have an eye for art and Hindu gods, Braedon commented.

The art is meant to distract his visitors so they don't notice his security measures, Raptor replied without visually acknowledging Braedon's silent question.

You mean like that small blur next to the tapestry on the left, which no doubt is the edge of a camouflage net, or the small gap behind that statue with the elephant head that probably houses a three hundred and sixty-degree camera? Braedon retorted, his own facial expression carefully neutral. *My point is that you can learn a lot about a person by studying their taste in art and entertainment.*

That sounds like something Steven would say.

It **was** *something Steven used to—*

Before Braedon could finish his thought, he suddenly felt the connection go dead. Raptor cast him a quick glance, his own features reflecting his shock. The loss of the implant feed left Braedon numb and momentarily disoriented. Based on the expressions on the faces of his companions, he knew that they were experiencing a similar effect.

"It's…it's gone!" Jade stammered. "I can't connect to the feed."

"Neither can I," Raptor confirmed. "Wait…where did our guide go?"

Braedon quickly studied his surroundings for signs of Lajvati, but to no avail. While he had been conversing with Raptor, their guide had led them through a set of doors into what appeared to be a large courtyard. Well-manicured shrubs and flowers lined two cobblestone pathways that wound further in. However, trees and plants of various sizes and shapes obscured the paths after about a dozen feet, leaving the guests to wonder as to their destination.

"The implant signal died the moment we stepped into the courtyard," Jade said. Retracing her steps, she walked over to the doors leading back into the mansion and attempted to open them. "Locked," she confirmed.

"Now what?" Braedon asked as Jade rejoined them.

For a moment, the three stood back to back and surveyed the area. Finally, Raptor broke the silence. "We follow the path."

"But which one?" Jade asked.

But before Raptor could reply, a voice echoed across the grounds. "If you value your life, don't make another move!"

The "guests" suddenly found themselves surrounded by six men, each throwing off the invisibility cloaks that had been concealing their presence from view. The burly men were dressed in military fatigues and each had his laser pistol pointed in the direction of the prisoners.

10

SACRIFICE

"Hey now, boys. Let's not get jumpy," Raptor said, his hands raised in the air. "We've got an appointment to see Sarbjeet. He's expecting us."

"All three of you, turn and face the path," one of the Hindu guards ordered as he took a step toward them, his English heavily accented.

As they complied, Braedon cast a concerned glance at Raptor. "I thought you said this Sarbjeet was a friend of yours."

"Well, he is…sort of," Raptor replied with a smirk. "In my business, the word *friend* is a rather loose term."

The men took up positions around them, two in the front, one on each side, and two behind them. Out of the six men, only the two in the back kept their weapons out.

"Follow me," the one in the front said as he began walking toward the path on the right.

Left with no options, Braedon and the others did as commanded. As they walked deeper into the secluded courtyard, Braedon turned his thoughts toward the others. *Do we try to take them out now? What's the plan?* However, after waiting several seconds for a reply, he remembered that the implant connection was not available. *Huh. I can't believe how reliant I'd become on this thing*, Braedon thought. *I guess we'll have to do it the old-fashioned way.* Turning his head slightly, he waited for a moment for Raptor to turn also so he could catch his eye.

As their eyes met, Braedon raised an eyebrow questioningly. By way of response, Raptor lowered his eyes briefly to focus on Braedon's left arm, which was still in the sling. Nodding almost imperceptibly to show that he understood, Braedon returned his gaze back to facing forward.

The guards led them through the undergrowth into a circular opening about forty feet in diameter with an elegant fountain in the middle that contained sculptures of Brahma, Vishnu, and Shiva. As they entered the area, Raptor spoke. "Listen, this has *got* to be a mistake. I've worked with Sarbjeet many times and—"

The guard in front stopped the group and turned around quickly, cutting off Raptor's words. "Then you know how he likes to do things," the guard said with a sly grin curling the corner of his mouth.

As if in reaction to the guard's words, Raptor took a deliberate step to his right, causing him to bump into Braedon's left arm.

Taking his cue, Braedon let out a cry of pain as he grabbed at his arm and doubled over. As he did so, he let the already loosened sling fall completely to the ground. In that moment, with the guards' attention focused on Braedon, Jade struck.

With one swift roundhouse kick, Jade knocked the weapons out of the hands of the two men in the back of the formation. Although her initial attack succeeded, her follow-up punch was blocked by the guard nearest her. Surprised by the quick recovery of her captors, Jade switched tactics. Dropping into a crouch, she swung her leg in the opposite direction and tripped the man behind her.

Due to the speed of Jade's attack, the guards reflexively switched the focus of their attention off Braedon. Using that to his advantage, Braedon rose up from his doubled-over position and swung his good, right arm into the chin of the man on his left. The swift uppercut sent the man sprawling to the path unconscious. Spinning around, Braedon kicked out at another one of the guards with his left leg. Anticipating the attack, the guard caught Braedon's foot with his hands and immediately began twisting his captive's trapped leg. Instinctively, Braedon rolled with the twist to avoid injury. As he did so, he pushed off the ground with his right foot, twisted his torso in the air, and planted his right foot into the face of his attacker. While the maneuver managed to cause the man to release his foot, it also left Braedon falling facedown onto the cobblestone path.

Meanwhile, next to him, Raptor grappled with one of the other guards. Although he lacked the martial arts skill of his companions, Raptor had nevertheless developed a brawling style of combat that served him well during his adolescent years of living on the street. Grabbing another of the guards by the head, he brought his knee up into the man's forehead. As he released the unconscious man, he felt a pair of muscular arms wrap themselves around him.

For several seconds, the two men struggled for control. Despite his best efforts, Raptor couldn't get any traction. The guard slowly pushed his opponent toward the fountain. Frantically, Raptor tried to head-butt his attacker, but to no avail. Then, just as the man was preparing to slam Raptor's head into one of the statues, his arms released their grip as his body slumped to the ground. Leaning over the edge of the fountain to catch his breath, Raptor watched helplessly as his rescuer, Jade took a blow to her abdomen from another attacker, knocking her backward.

Nearby, Braedon, whose lip was cut and bleeding, had regained his feet and was countering the blows of one of the other remaining guards.

Gathering his strength, Raptor looked around the area, frantically searching for the last of the guards. Finally, he located the outline of the man crouching off to the side of the path. As he stood, Raptor saw the unmistakable shape of a gun in his hand. "Braedon!" he yelled, knowing that his companion would be the only one who could possibly reach the man in time to stop him, if he could get away from his current attacker.

Upon hearing Raptor's warning, Braedon followed his gaze until he spotted the gun-wielding guard. However, the man's weapon was already pointed at Jade and ready to fire. Oblivious to the danger, Jade was still engaged with the other guard, who was retreating away from her.

With no other option available, Braedon broke off from his attacker and dove into the line of fire just as the guard's weapon discharged.

At the sound of the blast, Jade dropped to the ground and glanced behind her just in time to see Braedon hit the pathway, his body limp. A look of pure shock overcame Jade as she came to grips with what Braedon had just done for her.

"FREEZE!" the guard holding the pistol shouted at Jade and Raptor. Knowing they'd been defeated, the two companions stood slowly. "You three put on a good show, but the game's over. You lost. Now, step over to—"

Suddenly, before he could say another word, he was interrupted by a low rumble that began softly, then crescendoed rapidly.

For a brief instant, the three guards and their two prisoners froze in place as their minds sought to make sense of the new situation. Near the edge of the clearing, trees began to lean as the ground heaved beneath them. The cobblestone pathway split and cracked, forming fissures several inches wide. Finally registering the gravity of the situation, the group of former combatants scattered in search of cover. Far above them, a crevice formed in the ceiling of the cavern as the massive earthquake sent cascades of rock and debris raining down upon them and the citizens of Dehali.

11

SARBJEET

Rocks and dust continued to fall for several minutes after the earthquake subsided. And for nearly all that time, Jade and Raptor huddled under the nearby trees. Shortly after the earthquake had begun, the two of them managed to pull Braedon to safety while the three conscious guards did the same with their comrades. Once it was clear that the danger had passed, Raptor stood and glanced around the courtyard as if looking for something.

"Sarbjeet!" Raptor called out as he continued his visual search. "Sarbjeet! The game's over. It looks like we've all got bigger things to attend to."

Next to him, Braedon began to moan and stir. "He's coming around," Jade confirmed. "The effects of the stun blast are wearing off."

"Good," Raptor said as his eyes locked onto a group of approaching figures. "Sarbjeet's coming. We need to get him up." Standing to his feet, Raptor surveyed the damage from the earthquake as Sarbjeet and his entourage of guards drew closer.

Raptor's acquaintance, although only five feet, seven inches in height, and well over the age of fifty, still exuded such a strength and iron will that he commanded immediate respect and attention. In contrast to his confident, militaristic stride, he was dressed in an elegant shirt and matching pants typical of the Hindu ruling class instead of military fatigues, like his guards. The shirt and pants appeared mostly brown at first glance, but when studied closer, it became clear that the design was a mixture of tiny tan circles interwoven into a darker brown pattern. This design, mixed with the intricate embroidery around the cuffs, waist, and lapel, made for a striking image of finery.

"Kamal, I want the three of you to take Digvashta and the others to the infirmary, then report back here," Sarbjeet commanded as he pointed at the unconscious forms of his three downed guards. "And make it quick. It looks like we've got quite a bit of cleaning up to do."

As the men hurried off to do their commander's bidding, Sarbjeet turned his attention toward Raptor, Jade, and Braedon, who was just beginning to open his eyes. "Well, my old friend. You didn't do too bad. Three against six, and you still managed to disarm two of them and take out half of your opponents. My men are getting a little sloppy. Then again, you're new companion here," he said, giving Braedon a look of appraisal, "is quite the fighter. Your little sling trick no doubt caused my men to underestimate him."

Reaching out, Raptor shook the older man's hand firmly. "Yeah, he's not bad. He comes in handy once in a while," Raptor replied as Jade raised Braedon into a sitting position.

"He is a bit foolish, though," Sarbjeet commented. "You need to teach him a little about tactics. He wasted the chance to take down the shooter by jumping in front of the stun blast. If he had done that, he could have taken the pistol and you would have won. By taking the blast for Jade, you lost the game."

"Yeah, well, he's a little 'old-fashioned,'" Raptor said with a grin.

Sarbjeet was silent for a moment as he considered Raptor's comment. Then, as the truth dawned on him, a look of admiration and surprise crossed his features. "You didn't tell him, did you? He thought the pistol was set to kill and willingly sacrificed himself for Jade. Impressive," he stated as he looked down at Braedon with new respect.

"Wha…what's he…talking about?" Braedon murmured, his body still not cooperating fully.

"Nothing," Raptor replied. He helped Jade to get Braedon on his feet before continuing. "I'll tell you later. Anyway," he said, turning back to face their host, "how did you manage to shut down our implants like that?"

"Implant Disruptors," Sarbjeet stated, a triumphant grin on his face. "They're my latest 'toy.' Come into the house, all of you," he said as he started back down the path toward the mansion. The others quickly fell into step behind him, and as they walked, they suddenly felt the return of their implant feeds.

Walking confidently in front of his guests, Sarbjeet continued with the conversation. "In fact, the Disruptors are the whole reason that I wanted you to play my little 'game.' I wanted to see how well they'd work, as well as give my men some much needed practice, of course."

"Of course," Raptor echoed, his mind still digesting the import of this new information. "Do they affect everyone equally, or can you differentiate between targets?"

"Right now, they affect everyone in an area," Sarbjeet replied. "But we are hoping to be able to narrow the signal to be able to pinpoint specific targets."

"With everyone's reliance on implant technology, this could be *huge* in disrupting enemy communications," Raptor stated in genuine surprise. Glancing back at Jade, he saw that she understood the implication of this as well. "In fact, that's part of the reason we're here. We've come with some news that will be vital to the Dehali military. In return, we're asking that you help us to obtain some parts that we need."

"Yes, we'll get to that later," he said as they approached the doors leading back into the mansion. "Lajvati will help you to get settled. It seems that this latest earthquake has done more extensive damage than the one two standard weeks ago. I need to attend to these matters first, then you and I will talk."

"Understood," Raptor stated as the door to the mansion opened and Lajvati stood in the doorway waiting for them. As Sarbjeet headed off with his body guards into other portions of the mansion, Raptor turned to see that Jade and Braedon had fallen behind during the walk to the doors, the latter still recovering from the stun blast. Once they reached the doors, Lajvati led the trio into a hover-lift, which took them to the second floor. After exiting the lift, she escorted them down another exquisitely decorated hallway to one of several doors that lined the walls. As she drew near, the door opened automatically. Putting a delicate hand out, she ushered the visitors inside the guest room.

"When Mr. Saini is ready to see you, I will return," Lajvati said. "The door is not locked, but it would be… unwise to venture outside your room." Her message relayed to the guests, she headed back down the hallway, the door to the room closing immediately after her departure.

"Wow. Her enthusiasm is *so* infectious," Raptor said sarcastically as he turned around to face the others. "She—"

His words were suddenly cut off by the sight of Braedon standing in front of him, his furious expression mere inches from Raptor's face. "A game! That's all it was! And what? You thought it'd be hysterical to keep me in the dark? Or was this some kind of stupid test?"

Although Braedon was just over six feet in height, Raptor matched him inch for inch. His own flaring anger barely contained, Raptor met the other man's fiery gaze. "So what if I did? You're not part of my team! I don't have to tell you *anything*! I'm only helping you to save my *own* skin. And yes, as a matter of fact, it *was* sort of a test, and yes, I *did* find it *extremely* humorous!"

Quicker than he expected, Raptor felt Braedon's hands shoving him hard in the chest, the momentum sending him reeling into the wall. Rebounding, Raptor instinctively reached inside his jacket toward his weapon's holster, only to have his hand close over air. Remembering that he had to leave his pistol behind before entering Sarbjeet's mansion, he swore viciously.

Noticing his movement, Braedon grinned. "What's wrong? Don't want to fight me without your gun?"

Seething, Raptor prepared to leap upon the other when Jade appeared in front of him, her hand deftly knocking aside his clenched fist. "Stop this!" she commanded. "You two are acting like a couple of schoolgirls! This foolishness is getting us nowhere. We've got other matters to deal with. Charon's been trying to contact us and is practically ready to attack the mansion to find out what happened. On top of that, the news feeds are lighting up about the earthquake."

Jade's intervention succeeded in reducing the boiling tension down to a low simmer. "Fine," Raptor spat after several moments of brooding silence. "But let me tell you something, Christian. If you ever lay a hand on me again, the well will seem shallow compared to how deep *I'll* bury your body!"

Turning away from the confrontation, Raptor sat down heavily in one of the nearby chairs. Flicking on the room's holographic projector with a simple mental command, Raptor transferred the images coming into his implant from the Dehali news feeds to the device.

After several seconds, Braedon and Jade also sat down and became instantly mesmerized by the scenes unfolding on the holographic screen, all thoughts of the recent confrontation forgotten.

"By the Celestials, this one was the worst I've ever seen!" Jade remarked.

"Several entire blocks of the *Shudras* section were wiped out!" Braedon stated.

"Get in touch with our scientists. Make sure they're still safe," Raptor commanded. Nodding, Braedon activated his implant, his eyes momentarily losing focus as he communicated with Travis. Across the guest room, Raptor repeated the same actions as he contacted Charon and Xavier. Moments later, the two finished their private conversations. Raptor was the first to speak.

"Charon and Xavier are fine, but the Spelunker is going to need some repair and a new paint job. Did you get a hold of Travis?"

"Yeah. He and Gunther are okay, but he's extremely worried about his family," Braedon reported. "He spoke with his wife. They're safe for now, but their home was severely damaged. During the earthquake, they got pretty cut up and bruised."

"What about the temple? Any problems there?" Raptor asked.

"Not too much. A few cracks and minor damage," Braedon said.

"Contact Travis again, tell him I'm sending Xavier and Charon to go get his family now. Have him tell her to be ready," Raptor said, clearly agitated by the whole situation. "Just make sure he and Gunther keep working."

After another round of silent communications, Braedon and Raptor returned their attention to the news. "It wasn't just Dehali," Jade announced, her eyes glued to the screen. Switching the feed, she drew in her breath in shock, her normally guarded feelings exposing themselves.

"That's New China, isn't it?" Braedon asked, surprised by the sudden change in Jade's demeanor.

"Yes," she said, her voice laced with concern.

"Family?" Braedon asked softly.

"Two sisters."

Before Braedon could inquire further, the door to the room opened to reveal Lajvati standing in the entrance. "Mr. Saini will see you now, Mr. Ahmed."

Wincing slightly at the sound of his real surname, Raptor stood and looked over at Jade. "This shouldn't take too long." Turning, he exited the room.

Once the door was closed, Jade and Braedon refocused their attention on the news feed. As the scenes showed further destruction caused in New China, Braedon spoke,

"Jade, I don't know what you believe about God, but I want you to know that I'll be praying for your sisters."

Jade turned her head to face him, her eyes narrowed and her expression wary. "Why would you care anything about them? Don't give me some platitudes to make me feel better. There's too much pain in this world for me to believe that any god would care, much less intervene, on my behalf."

"Well, I *do* believe he cares," Braedon replied.

For several seconds, Jade didn't respond, but he simply turned back to face the holographic images. When she did finally speak, she didn't even look at him. "Why were you willing to sacrifice your own life to save me?" she asked, her voice an odd mixture of confusion and irritation. "What were you trying to prove?"

Braedon sat silent for several moments as he considered how best to respond. "I believe that God calls us to do what we can to save lives. I…I acted on instinct. I guess… You know, Jade, I don't fear death because I'm convinced that when I die, I'll be welcomed by God into heaven. But…but if *you* die, then…"

"Oh, I get it," she said with a snide grin. "To you I'm some lost…charity case…a sinner, so I'd wind up in hell. Right? How noble of you."

Letting out a sigh, Braedon responded, his voice low. "We're all sinners, Jade. I'm just as bad as you, Raptor, or anyone else. I'm just one beggar telling another where to find food."

Silence hung in the room for a few more minutes as Jade watched the news, completely ignoring Braedon's very presence. Finally, he noticed a slight movement of her head as she turned in his direction.

"No one has ever done anything like that for me," Jade said, breaking the silence with the soft tones of her voice. "Thank you."

"You're welcome," Braedon said simply. Without another word, the two of them turned their attention back to the holographic screen filled with images of the wreckage and destruction caused by the earthquake.

12

QUESTIONS AND ANSWERS

"This is worse than we had anticipated."

Sarbjeet paced the floor of the richly-furnished office room in which he and Raptor occupied. "We knew about the abominable practices Governor Mathison was dabbling with to create the various types of Guardians, and we knew he was messing around with the implant technology, but… to mind control his own people and use them as weapons? That's just…sickening," Sarbjeet spat out the words as if their very presence in his mouth made him want to vomit.

"Which is why your Implant Disruptors can be such a powerful tool against him," Raptor replied.

The Hindu man stopped his pacing for a moment as he considered everything he'd been told. Finally, he turned to face his companion. "This makes sense considering the types of materials he had been purchasing from me over the years. However, before I take this to General Ranjit, are you absolutely certain that this is his plan? How reliable is your source?"

"Extremely," Raptor replied. "In fact, I'm in possession of original documents that were taken by an insider from Mathison's own research facility."

"I will need a copy of those documents," Sarbjeet said, his eyes lit with an inner fire.

"Of course. In exchange, I was hoping you could supply us with a few items," Raptor replied.

"Let me see your list," Sarbjeet said as he sat down on the plush couch opposite his guest. With barely more than a twitch of his eye, Raptor transmitted the list over the implant connection to his companion, who studied it using his personal internal imaging system. "Yes, I can get them," the weapon's dealer said at last as he took a long drink from a glass sitting on his office desk. "But these aren't your standard-grade military parts. May I ask what you're going to use them for?"

"You may ask," Raptor quipped.

Sarbjeet didn't seem amused. "Rahib, don't play your games with me. There's a part of me that wonders if perhaps you aren't really still working for Mathison. Maybe you came here, pretending to be on the outs with your boss so that you can sell me false information."

The sudden coldness in Sarbjeet's tone sapped any remaining camaraderie Raptor may have felt. "To what end," he replied. Although he was outwardly calm, his heart began to beat faster at the change in the conversation.

Taking a step closer, Sarbjeet narrowed his eyes. "To get whatever parts you need while at the same time throwing us off the trail of what Mathison's *truly* working on."

Raptor grinned roguishly as he sat down on one of the plush chairs, his appearance calm and confident. Grabbing his own drink off the nearby table, he took a swig before responding. "You know that's a bunch of *griblin* squat. You've got eyes and ears everywhere. You know that the ESF has been hunting for my team, and that we had an encounter at the Om Hotel a couple of days ago. And you also know that a group of Guardians is heading toward Dehali as we speak."

After a few tense seconds, Sarbjeet's demeanor reverted back to its original professional level. "Yes," he acknowledged with a sigh. "I know you too well. It's obvious that you've gotten in over your head on this one. But if all of that's true, then it also means that the bounty that Mathison has placed on you is real. Tell me why I shouldn't just turn you in and collect on it? What else are you hiding?"

"Look, I came to you because I trust you *not* to turn me in or involve the Dehali Military," Raptor stated. "Let's just leave it with this: in addition to stealing some of his top-secret data, I also borrowed one of his key scientific researchers. He wants him back. So there you go. Now are you going to help me or not?"

There was a lull in the conversation as Sarbjeet deliberated with himself. Having reached a decision, he walked over to his desk and sat down in his office chair. "I don't like being left out of the loop, Rahib. I'll help this time. But *only* because I owe you for saving my life last year. I consider this payment for that debt. Next time, if there *is* a next time, I may not be so generous."

"Understood," Raptor stated, thankful that the conversation had returned to more solid ground. "How long do you think it'll take to get these parts?"

Sarbjeet studied the list again. "It will probably take a day or two, maybe three to get them all delivered to you, assuming you're staying somewhere here in the city."

Raptor nodded. "Could we get them any sooner if we pick them up?"

Sarbjeet shrugged. "Yes, I suppose that would work. In a hurry, huh? I'm assuming you hope to be gone from the city before the Guardians arrive."

"Something like that," Raptor replied.

"I'll send you details on how to find my supplier and specific instructions on how to work the deal," Sarbjeet said, his mind working rapidly. "Especially with the ESF sniffing around, I don't want to take any chances."

"Thanks, Sarbjeet. I knew I could count on you," Raptor said as he stood, preparing to leave.

Leaning back in his deluxe office chair, Sarbjeet acknowledged the gratitude with a slight nod of his head. "Good luck. Whatever you've gotten yourself into, I hope it doesn't get you killed. I'd hate to see you be reincarnated as a rat."

Raptor grinned slyly. "I don't think that'd work too well. I'm not overly fond of cheese. Who do I need to contact about getting my next life upgraded?"

His host laughed at the response. "Ha. If only it were that easy. You can't bribe *karma!*"

Although Raptor tried to brush off the comment, he could help but be reminded of Steven's prophecy regarding his impending demise. Sitting back down, Raptor leaned back in the chair, doing his best to appear casual as he responded. "Let me ask you something, do you really believe in reincarnation?"

His curiosity piqued by Raptor's question, Sarbjeet sat forward. "Yes, of course. Why do you ask?"

"I don't know," Raptor mumbled, his own mind asking himself the same question.

"What's wrong? Has the Christian gotten under your skin?"

"How did you know he was a…" Raptor frowned briefly before the truth struck him. "So you overheard our little… disagreement. Well, hopefully I won't be subjected to his insane prattle for too much longer."

Sarbjeet laughed. "Let me guess, he tried to 'convert' you."

Raptor shrugged. "I suppose you could say that. I will say, though, that he has a unique approach. Instead of just spewing his religious dogma in my face, he's challenged me to put all religions 'on trial,' as if that were even possible."

"Interesting," Raptor's host said in genuine interest. "How does he propose to do that?"

"For starters, he says everyone should attempt to figure out what each religion teaches in order to determine if it's even *possible* to 'prove' if it's true or not. I don't know if he made them up or not, but he's got four questions that he uses to summarize a religion's teachings."

Raptor studied the other man's reaction to determine if he should continue. To his surprise, Sarbjeet seemed completely engaged in the topic.

"What are the questions?" Sarbjeet asked. "Do you remember them?"

Pausing, Raptor searched through his memories of his previous conversations with Braedon. "I know for sure that the first one was about the origin of the universe. Something like…'Where did humans come from?' Then there was a question about what happens when we die. The other two were…something about suffering and evil. 'Why is there suffering?' and 'How do we fix things?' I think."

Sarbjeet leaned back in his chair again as he considered the questions. "And what does this mighty sage say you should do after that?"

"I don't know," Raptor said nonchalantly. "He also thinks people should examine how each of the religions began. Like most exclusivist religious zealots, he's been brainwashed into believing that his religion is the only *true* religion and that everyone else is wrong. The arrogance of that just..."

Frustrated, Raptor let his thought remain unfinished. Across from where he was sitting, Sarbjeet chuckled. "Someday I would love to hear the story of how the two of you ended up working together."

Despite his irritation with Braedon's beliefs, Raptor couldn't help but let out a chuckle of his own. "Yeah. It's quite a tale."

"I will say this about your friend: he's obviously given this whole thing a lot of thought," Sarbjeet commented. "I'm surprised that you would even bother to get into conversations about religion. Why the sudden interest?"

"Let's just say I've had one too many brushes with death," Raptor said, dodging the question. "You know me. I've never had time for religion. But...I guess recent events have got me thinking."

Sarbjeet picked up his glass and took another drink of its contents. "I've been surrounded by Hinduism all my life, and I can tell you that I find it to be very helpful. Have you considered it?"

Raptor shook his head. "I hadn't gotten that far. We've only discussed Buddhism. Aren't the two similar?"

"Only in the sense that they both believe in reincarnation, and that Buddha himself was a Hindu," Sarbjeet replied. "Hinduism is basically a group of religions and cultures that developed over thousands of years. It is a way of life. That's why it has become so strong here in Tartarus. Those who arrived from Earth's Hindu population couldn't help but continue the religion."

"So how did Hinduism get started on Earth?"

"As far as I know, no one knows how it got started," Sarbjeet said.

"What about Braedon's four questions?" Raptor asked. "How would you answer those?"

Sarbjeet gave a mild laugh. "I can do my best, but I'm not a *Brahmin*, of course. The first question is easy: like reincarnation, the universe is born, expands for billions of years, then contracts, only to repeat this cycle over and over again. There is no beginning or end."

Raptor frowned. "But where did all the matter in the universe come from? Who created it?"

"No one 'created' it. It is all part of the supreme Brahman."

"Is Brahman the same as God?" Raptor asked, his confusion deepening.

"Yes, but not like the God of Christians or Jews," Sarbjeet said. "In Hinduism, everything is part of Brahman."

"But I noticed on the way in that you have tons of statues of various gods," Raptor said, pointing to a statue sitting on the shelf of the office for emphasis. "I don't get it. Do you worship one god, or many gods?"

Sarbjeet smiled. "I'm glad you liked my collection. The answer to your question is yes."

"Yes what?"

"Yes. We serve one 'god' who is made up of many gods."

"So I'm part of god, and you're a part of god?" Raptor asked.

Sarbjeet nodded. "Let me explain using a famous Hindu story. There was once a king who ruled over the Land of the Blind. An elephant came to this land, and the king sent his courtiers to find out about this strange animal. They each touched a different part of the animal and described it to the king. The one who touched the elephant's side said that it was 'like a wall.' The one who touched the tusk said it was 'like a spear,' The man who touched the ear said it was 'like a fan.' Another touched the leg and said it was 'like a tree.' Yet another touched the trunk and said it was 'like a snake.' Finally, the last man touched the tail and said it was 'like a rope.'

"You see," Sarbjeet continued, "all the men were right, but only in part."

"I suppose Brahman represents the elephant, and the thousands of gods represent different parts of Brahman," Raptor summarized.

"Exactly," Sarbjeet said. "And we all become a part of Brahman once we achieve *moksha*."

"*Moksha?*" Raptor echoed. "What's that?"

"It is liberation from the cycle of birth, death, and rebirth," Sarbjeet replied.

"Isn't that the same as the Buddhist concept of *nirvana?*" Raptor asked.

"Mostly," Sarbjeet said. "There are slight differences, depending on who you ask."

"And how does *karma* play into all of this?"

"Simple. When you live rightly or follow the *dharma*, you will gain good *karma*, and good things will happen to you in the future," Sarbjeet explained. "But if you do bad things, then bad will happen to you."

Raptor felt a sudden emptiness in the pit of his stomach. "So if your good deeds outweigh your bad, then you get to be reincarnated at a higher level. But if your bad deeds are greater, then you are reborn at a lower level, perhaps even an animal, like a rat."

With their previous banter giving way to the more serious conversation, Sarbjeet considered Raptor's situation. "I'm afraid so. But if you start doing good now, you may yet have time left before you die to tip the scales in your favor."

Thinking back to Steven's prophecy, Raptor felt fear tear into his soul. "Maybe," he muttered. "So if I understand this correctly, the universe is in an endless cycle of creation and destruction that lasts billions of year, suffering is the result of bad *karma*, we make things better by following a set of rules called *dharma*, and the ultimate goal in life is to cease to exist by becoming part of Brahman."

"Obviously that's an oversimplification of things," Sarbjeet stated. "But in essence it's true."

Taking one last drink from his glass, Raptor stood. "Look, I've gotta run. As much as I've enjoyed our conversation, if I don't get going, Jade will give me an earful for making her wait so long."

Sarbjeet nodded, sensing that their conversation had left his friend unsettled. "It's good to see you again, Rahib. Take care of yourself. I'll have Lajvati show you and your friends out, and your car will be waiting for you."

"Thanks again, Sarbjeet," Raptor said as he headed for the door, his mind still swirling with thoughts of *karma*, Brahman, and hopelessness.

Yeah, what do you want?

Mr. Moravec, I am calling with information that will be valuable to you.

And what might that be?

You are offering a reward for information regarding the whereabouts of your brother, Caleb, and his friends, are you not?

Marcel set down his drink and sat up straight, his eyes igniting with burning hatred. *Have you seen him? Where are they?*

He listened intently for a moment to the voice coming through his implant. Slowly, a wicked grin spread across his features. Closing down the connection, he jumped to his feet and yelled out a command to his cohorts sitting nearby. "Grab your gear, boys! We've got an appointment to keep. In Dehali!"

13

Tact and Charm

Xavier, we're here, Raptor said through the teleconnect. *How long before you guys arrive?*

We're right behind ya, boss. We just dropped off Travis's family, and we're leaving the temple now. We'll be there in about…oh, ten minutes or so. That is, unless Charon decides to stop for ice cream or something.

Raptor suppressed a chuckle brought on by the uncharacteristic mental picture. *Good. The sooner we get these parts to Gunther and Travis, the better,* Raptor stated. *TC me when you get here.*

You got it.

Closing down the connection, Raptor focused on driving the Obsidian. Neither Jade or Braedon said a word as he turned the black hovercar onto the private roadway that led to the warehouse. Pulling up to the double-wide main gate, Raptor rolled down the window. Remembering Sarbjeet's explicit instructions, he activated the communicator that sat on a pedestal near the gate. "My name is Rahib. I'm here to pick up an order that was called in by the

Brigadier. Ganesha smiles with favor upon my enterprise," Raptor said, repeating the special code phrase.

Several seconds passed, leaving the trio of visitors nothing to do but stare disconcertedly at the numerous camera mounts and weapons placements that had clearly locked onto their vehicle.

Finally, a voice came through the device. "You may enter," it said abruptly as the double gates slid open. "Please proceed to your preassigned docking bay."

"Thank you," Raptor said. He rolled up his window as he pressed the accelerator, easing the car into the large warehouse courtyard. Although he often used the car's automatic driver, he liked to maintain control when moving into unknown territories. "Braedon, once the others arrive, Xavier and Charon will take you to meet with your Crimson Liberty friends. We need to get that cash you promised."

"I've already contacted them," the soldier replied from the back seat. "I'll talk to them, but I'm not promising anything. And I don't need an escort. Why not just let me take the Obsidian and the rest of you can ride in the Spelunker?"

"Because I don't think you're terrorist friends would be too happy with you if you revealed their location to Sarbjeet or any of his military connections," Raptor replied snidely.

"Sarbjeet put a tracker on our car?" Braedon responded in surprise, letting the jibe about his friends being "terrorists" slide. "But I thought you trusted him?"

"Trust is a very loose term," Raptor stated. "Besides, I'm not sure it was by his order. It's possible someone else who works for him did it. Anyway, I don't want them to know just yet that we're aware of its existence. So Xavier and

Charon will take you while we get the parts we need. We'll meet you back at the temple when you're done."

"Fine, then let me take the Spelunker," Braedon shot back. "I don't need babysitters."

"I don't think any of us should be out by ourselves," Raptor stated, his irritation rising.

"Why don't you just say what you're thinking—you don't trust me," Braedon said, his own frustration building.

"Okay, I don't trust you," Raptor spat. "Does that make you feel better? You got me to admit the truth. And you're all about truth, aren't you?"

Although Braedon couldn't see the other man's expression, something in his tone of voice left him with the impression that he was hiding something. This criminal had some other reason for wanting the other two to tag along, but unfortunately, Braedon wasn't in any position to prevent them from doing so. Letting the conversation die, he turned his attention back to the window.

Raptor drove the vehicle up to the assigned loading dock and brought it to a stop. Shutting off the engine, he, Braedon, and Jade exited the car, careful to keep their hands in clear sight per Sarbjeet's instructions.

The moment it was clear that the newcomers were unarmed, five men stepped through the small door next to the bay. Climbing the short set of stairs that led up to the main floor of the warehouse, Raptor smiled at the wary men. Recognizing the one in front from the photo Sarbjeet sent him, Raptor held out a hand in greeting. "Mr. Desai, it's a pleasure to meet you."

"Yes," the Hindu man replied, the inflection of his voice flat. "I received your order from the Brigadier. He requested that I put a rush on it, but all of my service droids are busy fulfilling another order at this time. I'll pull a couple of them off the previous job, but that's all I can spare. I should have everything ready in about ninety minutes."

"That'll be fine," Raptor replied. "However, I hope it won't be a problem, but my colleague here," he said, pointing to Braedon, "has other business to attend to and will have to leave shortly."

Mr. Desai glanced quickly at Braedon. "He can exit through the main gate. You and the woman will wait here until we are ready to load your vehicle." Without another word, the men disappeared back through the door.

"Friendly bunch," Jade stated sarcastically.

"Well, I guess we just sit in the car and wait," Raptor stated as he headed back toward the Obsidian. Jade and Braedon followed suit, and soon, the three of them were back in the vehicle.

After several minutes, Raptor received a message from Xavier. "Charon and Xavier are outside the gate," he said to Braedon. "Don't take too long. We need that money to purchase supplies."

"Don't worry, Mommy," Braedon quipped as he opened the door, "I'll be back soon." Climbing out of the car, Braedon closed the door and headed toward the gate.

In the passenger seat, Jade stifled a grin. Noticing his companion's reaction, Raptor feigned indignance. "What?"

Jade turned toward him. "He's right, you know. You do act like a mother hen sometimes."

"Shut up," Raptor stated as he looked away in order to hide his own lopsided smile.

"This is it?" Charon said, the disdain in his voice clearly heard in each word. "What a dump!"

Braedon looked out the window of the Spelunker and over at the dilapidated house and found that, for once, he agreed with Charon. The building appeared to be left over from the early days of the founding of the colony. Weeds and vines ran amuck, the windows were filmy, and the exterior probably hadn't seen any attention for at least fifty years.

Which is why it was perfect for their meeting place.

"Yeah, its almost as bad as the places you and Raptor have had us hiding out in," Braedon said, the dig spilling out of his mouth before his better judgment could stop himself from antagonizing the burly man.

Sure enough, Charon bristled at the comment, his short temper beginning to flare. Recognizing that his partner's already short fuse just lost another inch, Xavier spoke up quickly.

"It doesn't even look like anybody even lives here."

The con man's tactic was marginally successful. Forgetting the initial slight, Charon focused on a new irritant. "That's because they probably don't," he said, casting a baleful glance at Braedon, who sat in the back seat of the vehicle. "This is just a safe house or something, isn't it, soldier boy?"

Braedon nodded, his expression neutral.

Charon harrumphed. "You come across as all 'high and mighty,' but you Christians are just like us 'lowlifes.' You don't trust me and Xavier with the location of one of their real hideouts, so you set up the meeting somewhere else. Ha!" he spat. "And here I thought you Christians were supposed to trust others. What a bunch of hypocrites!"

Having expected the tirade, Braedon met the man's gaze with a calm acceptance. "Charon, you're mistaken. Nowhere in the Bible are Christians commanded to trust others. 'Love' yes, but 'trust'? That's gotta be earned. As a matter of fact, Jesus told his disciples to be as 'cunning as a snake and as innocent as a dove.'"

His eyes narrowing, Charon glared over his shoulder at the other man. "Let's get something straight: Raptor puts up with you because he thinks you can be useful. But I don't agree. If anything even so much as *smells* out of place here, I'm pulling the plug on this operation. You can stay here and rot with the rest of your rodent pals for all I care."

"Well then, this shouldn't take long," Xavier commented dryly. Noting Charon's confused and impatient expression, Xavier elaborated. "You said that if anything 'smells' out of place, we're gone, right? Well, based on the looks of that place, something is *bound* to smell!"

Charon backhanded Xavier across his nearest shoulder. "I'm gonna have a little talk with Raptor," the big man said, mostly to himself. "This is the *last* time I get stuck with either of these two." Shoving open the door of the Spelunker, he growled at the others. "C'mon. Let's get this over with."

Despite the soreness in his shoulder caused by Charon's outburst, Xavier grinned. "Don't worry," he said to Braedon as he reached for the door handle, "he grows on ya."

Stifling a chuckle, Braedon shook his head and opened his own door. Once outside the vehicle, the three men quickly crossed the few short feet from the curb to the front door. As they approached, the door swung open, seemingly of its own accord. Just inside the darkened doorway, a shadowy figure beckoned for them to enter. The moment

Braedon and the others were inside, their host closed the door and turned to face them.

"Braedon, it's so good to see you again!"

As their eyes adjusted to the dim interior of the building, Xavier and Charon looked with mild surprise as the speaker embraced Braedon.

"You too, Kianna," Braedon replied warmly. "I see you're growing out your hair. It looks nice."

The dark-skinned woman smiled as she brushed a long strand of her curly, black hair out of her face. Although she was in her late thirties, she still retained the beauty of a woman much younger. "Thanks. You look the same as ever. And still getting into trouble, I see," she said with a smirk as she shifted her gaze toward her other two guests. "Hi, I'm Kianna," she stated as she held out her hand toward Xavier.

However, instead of shaking it, the actor deftly pivoted the hand in his own, exposing her knuckles. Leaning over, he kissed them gently, his eyes never leaving hers. "It is a distinct pleasure to meet you," he said suavely. Standing next to him, Charon rolled his eyes and let out a grunt of impatience.

For her part, Kianna laughed lightheartedly as she tossed a questioning glance in Braedon's direction. "Well, thank you, mister…"

"Xavier," he stated. "Xavier Traverse."

"It's a pleasure to meet you, Xavier," Kianna said. "Now, may I have my hand back? If you're finished with it, that is."

Releasing her hand, Xavier smiled and winked. "Of course, *mon cheri.*"

Amused at the younger man's gesture, Kianna turned her attention toward Charon. However, when she reached out to shake his hand, he deliberately stepped past her and began heading toward the interior of the house. "Where's everyone else?" Charon stated as his eyes searched the barren living room for signs that the place was occupied. "You said we were meeting your 'friends'—plural," he continued, turning back around to face Braedon. "Or did you deceive us about that as well?"

"No, Charon," said a new voice, "there are indeed others here."

Spinning back around and dropping into a defensive crouch, Charon wiped out his gun and pointed it at the newcomer standing in the doorway leading into the kitchen area. Like the majority of the population of Dehali, the man was of Hindu descent and dressed in a colorful tunic and pants of green, with silver embroidery along the edges. Slight traces of silver could be seen streaking through the man's jet-black hair, leaving Charon to guess that he was in his early fifties. Noting that the man leaned heavily on a wooden cane, and considering that he only came up to Charon's chin, the burly man relaxed his posture and drew himself up to his full height, his shoulder-length blond hair swinging slightly with the motion.

"And who are you?" Charon demanded, his eyes narrowing.

"I am Manoj," he said, his English accent noticeable but not overly distracting. "I am the leader of the Crimson Liberty cell here in Dehali. It is a pleasure to—"

"Let's cut to the chase," Charon said rudely. "I don't like surprises, so I suggest you don't *ever* do that again, or you might find yourself filled with several new holes in inconvenient places. And if anyone else is creeping around here, I'd recommend you warn them as well. Also, in case you hadn't noticed, I don't play well with others," he said with a sneer. "So if you and the princess over here," he said, gesturing toward Kianna, "would finish your business with Braedon, we can be on our merry way. Do you got it, or do I need to spell it out for you?"

"You know, Charon, you've got about as much tact and charm as a pile of three-week-old *Bandilo* spaghetti," Xavier said as he crossed over to stand next to Charon. "And you wonder why Raptor never lets you do any negotiating. Sorry about that, Manoj. It really is nice to meet you. Nice place you've got here," he said in jest as he glanced around the dusty room.

Undeterred by Charon's gruffness, Manoj acknowledged Xavier's courtesy with a nod then addressed his larger partner, the dim lighting of the room serving to enhance the look of empathy on the older man's face. "I promise you, Charon, we will not be long. It is a shame that you are in such a hurry to leave. Despite what you may think, you are here among friends."

Charon harrumphed but didn't respond.

"Anyway, if you'd follow me, I'll take you downstairs to meet the others," Manoj continued. "Then we can talk." Turning, he led the group further into the house then down a flight of decrepit stairs that led into a dank basement. However, once they crossed the threshold into the main living area, Braedon and his companions were surprised to find the place well furnished and well maintained. In fact, the effect was like stepping into a completely different modern building.

Sitting at a long table were a group of three men and a woman, each appearing to be just beyond their mid-twenties. As the party entered the room, they stood up from their holographic display screens and greeted Braedon and

Xavier. Although they attempted to greet Charon as well, a warning glare from him served to quell their enthusiasm.

"Hridya, Darpan, Tanak, and Kirtan have all been working closely with Kianna on shutting down the human trafficking ring," Manoj said once they had all assembled in the room. "In the past several months, we've finally been able to locate the tunnel that the smugglers use to get their victims out of Dehali."

Charon cleared his throat loudly. "That's all *very* interesting," he said, his voice oozing sarcasm. "But can we get to the topic at hand?"

Bristling, Braedon glared at Charon, their eyes locking. Not wanting the situation to dissolve into a fight, Braedon took a deep breath to calm himself before speaking. "Look, Charon, you've made it abundantly clear that you don't want to be here. But this is my turf. You're not calling the shots right now. So just back off. We'll get out of here as soon as possible. In the meantime, sit down and relax for once."

For several seconds, the tension in the air paralyzed everyone in the room as the two men continued their staring contest. Finally, Charon nodded almost imperceptibly then glanced around the room as he turned away. "Do you have anything to drink around here that's *not* water?"

As Charon eased his thick frame onto a nearby couch, Darpan grabbed a beverage from the cooling unit and nervously handed it to him.

"Wow. That was fun," Xavier said, a look of relief on his face. "For a moment there, I thought I might have to step in and save Charon from a first-class whooping," he whispered to Kianna. Laughing at the remark, she grinned at Xavier.

"Darpan, would you please grab Xavier and Braedon something to drink as well?" she said as she motioned for Xavier to sit at one of the other chairs nearby.

Happy to have something else to do to get him away from Charon, Darpan gladly complied. While he did so, Braedon addressed Charon and Xavier. "I need to talk to Manoj and Kianna privately."

"What?" Charon said angrily. "You never said anything about—"

He stopped mid-sentence as a message came through his implant. His eyes lost their focus for a second, and when they refocused, his anger began to dissipate. "Fine. Let's just get this over with."

Turning to look at Kianna and Manoj, Braedon nodded for them to proceed. Taking their cue, they led Braedon to an adjoining room and closed the door behind them. After a few awkward seconds of silence, Xavier looked around at the others in the room and smiled. "So...anyone up for a game of poker?"

14

AMONG FRIENDS

"Okay, I can't *wait* to hear this story. Where in Tartarus did you meet *those* two?"

Braedon rolled his eyes and shook his head in response to Kianna's question. "If you think *they're* bad, you should meet Raptor and Jade. Honestly, have you ever been sure you're in God's will, but you just can't figure out what he could *possibly* be doing?"

"Yes, all the time," Manoj said as he pulled out a chair from the lone table and sat down, indicating for the others to do so also. "His ways are *definitely* not our ways."

"So where *did* you meet them anyway?" Kianna said, more seriously.

Braedon proceeded to explain all that had happened to him since first meeting Gunther. When he mentioned Steven's death, he saw his own grief reflected in their eyes.

"It broke my heart to hear of his death," Manoj stated softly. "After he was framed, he needed a place to go for awhile and came here. He had many questions and needed support. I did what I could to help him get back on his feet. He was a good friend."

For a moment, silence reigned in the small room as each of them became lost in memories of their departed friend. Finally, Braedon broke the silence. "He was like a father to me. He took me in when I first arrived in Dehali ten years ago. If it hadn't been for him…I…I'm not sure I would have made it. I don't know if either of you know what it's like to leave behind a spouse and a whole other life."

Kianna looked down at the wedding ring on Braedon's finger. "Your wife…she's back on Earth?"

"Yes. We were traveling on vacation. She was near me when the portal appeared, but… I was the only one that got pulled through."

"I'm sorry," Kianna said.

Braedon pursed his lips. "Since I wasn't Hindu, the people at the Dehali Welcome Center suggested I be transferred to Elysium. There I met Steven, and he…he helped me overcome my depression. Now, I want to do everything I can to honor his memory by trying to complete what he started."

Manoj narrowed his eyes in curiosity. "Do you really believe that this scientist…Gunt…"

"Gunther," Braedon corrected.

"Gunther can really reverse the portals and open up a gateway to Earth?" Manoj asked, his expression an odd mixture of doubt and hope.

"I think he's got a better chance than most," Braedon replied. "I saw firsthand what that device of his can do. If he could just harness the energy and get it focused…yeah. I think he can do it."

Kianna leaned in slightly as she studied the soldier's features. "And are you willing to *die* to help him?"

Braedon paused for just a second before answering her question. "Yes, I am. Steven thought the chance was worth it, and so do I."

"But the more important question is, do you feel that this is something *God* wants you to do?" Manoj asked, his tone serious. "Have you sought *his* counsel on this?"

"Yes, I have," Braedon nodded. "I'm not sure what part I have in all this, but I feel that things are beginning to happen in Tartarus that are bigger than Mathison…bigger than any of us. Events are building. Before long, something is going to explode. Which is why I've come here tonight. We need your help."

"We gathered that much based on your message," Kianna said as she leaned back in her chair. "What can we do?"

"Well, for starters, we need some funds," Braedon began. "We had to purchase several pieces of equipment that Gunther needs to finish his machine, and based on what I've seen of the seller, if we don't pay for those parts real soon, it won't matter if the machine works because we won't live long enough to use it."

Manoj frowned. "I see. How much do you need?"

A muscle in Braedon's cheek twitched as he braced himself for their response. "Twenty thousand credits."

Kianna and Manoj both stared at him in shock. After a moment, Manoj recovered enough to complete a full sentence. "But that's…that's almost everything that we've managed to scrape together. If we…even if we gave you half of that, it would set us back months if not…if not *years* in our efforts. We need that money to continue our fight against this vile slave trade."

Braedon leaned in, his expression firm. "But don't you see? If we succeed in opening the portals back to Earth, it would *end* the slave trade here because there wouldn't be anyone left in Tartarus. Everyone could return to Earth."

"More than that," Kianna added, "the way things are going with all of these earthquakes and stuff, I'm not sure Tartarus will *survive* that much longer."

"What do you mean?" Braedon asked, shiver running down his spine at her words.

"We've only heard rumors, but they seem to match what we've been seeing in the news from every territory," Kianna continued. "From what we've been able to gather, some scientists are beginning to worry that this world is becoming unstable. There has been an increase in geological movements that are causing larger and more frequent earthquakes, like the one we saw earlier today. The major governments have been keeping a tight lid on the reports, but we're concerned that if this is true, we all may not have long."

Braedon sat in stunned silence for several seconds before responding. "That would explain why that pack of *svith* attacked us in the Fringe. Whatever it is that's causing the earthquakes must have driven them from their normal nesting grounds."

"Whether it is true or not," Manoj interjected, "the more immediate question is, even if we give you the funds to pay for the parts, what then? When does your scientist expect to have the machine ready?"

"He says it should only take a couple of days. And actually, that's the other little thing we need help with," Braedon said. "According to Gunther, once the machine is completed, it needs to be calibrated. In order to do that, he needs to get some readings from an *open portal.*"

Kianna let out a loud laugh. "Are you serious? Don't tell me you're gonna to try to sneak into the Dehali Welcome Center! Oh, Lord! Y'all are crazy!"

"Well, unless you've got another active portal tucked away somewhere that I don't know about, that's our only choice," Braedon replied matter-of-factly. "Besides, Raptor and his gang are pretty competent when it comes to breaking into places unnoticed."

Kianna snorted softly. "Yeah, I bet!"

"So what can we do to help," Manoj said, bringing the focus back to the immediate issue.

"We could use any information you have on the Center itself. Access points, schematic layouts, blueprints, security, etc.," Braedon said.

Becoming more serious, Kianna shrugged. "That shouldn't be too hard. We've been gathering intel on that place for quite some time to try to figure out how they've been smuggling the people out to sell them at other cities."

"Yes, and we just recently discovered the answer to that puzzle," Manoj added.

Kianna's features darkened. "Yeah, the slimeballs have a hidden passageway that leads out and away from the city. It's kept completely hidden from the general populace."

Braedon sat silent for a moment as he contemplated this new piece of information. "This could come in handy. We'll take whatever info you can provide. Also," he said, turning his full attention to Kianna, "I was hoping you might be able to provide us with some technical assistance."

"What did you have in mind?" Kianna said, intrigued.

"If you're not too busy, maybe you could use those 'finely toned' computer hacking skills to help us gain access to the Welcome Center."

Kianna raised an eyebrow. "Fake access codes and digital IDs? That could be quite the challenge."

"It would certainly go a long way in helping us get in," Braedon said. "I'm not sure what else Raptor may have up his sleeve, but I would certainly feel much better knowing I had someone I could truly trust at my back. Right now, Raptor and I have a common goal, but I don't trust him."

"I don't blame you," Manoj said. "Based on how you've described him and his team, you might be better off without him."

Braedon shook his head. "No. Not right now. As I mentioned, they definitely have a skill set that is vital to pulling off this job. I'm not sure why, but I believe God has us working together for a reason."

"Uh-huh," Kianna smirked. "That big guy out there looks like he could take down a whole army of sentry droids bare-handed! Speaking of 'Hercules,' how come he suddenly backed down out there?" Kianna asked. "I thought he was going to blow a gasket or something, and then… poof…he just gave up. The way he glazed over, he must have gotten a message from someone."

Braedon grinned. "I figured he might have a problem with us going off alone, so I contacted his buddy, Raptor, and asked him to intervene. Obviously, he agreed with my reasoning and called off his bulldog."

"Nice," Kianna added.

"We trust your judgment in this, Braedon," Manoj said. "It's clear to me that God has his hand upon you. I earnestly hope and pray that you'll be successful. I'll talk to the others about your financial needs. I'll get back to you as soon as I receive word."

"Understood," Braedon said as he stood. "I would've expected nothing less. Thank you."

"All for His kingdom," Manoj replied as he and Kianna both followed suit and stood. Turning to look at her, he continued, "It appears that your other duties will have to wait. I'll get Hridya and Kirtan to cover for you in the meantime. Perhaps Tanak could go with you to help. He's quite knowledgeable about government procedures and protocol. I wish I could do more, but we still have many other pressing matters that require our attention and resources."

"Thank you again," Braedon said as he reached out and grasped the other's hand.

"Before you leave, do me the honor of allowing me to pray for you both," Manoj said.

As the three of them bowed their heads, Manoj's strong voice filled the room even as his words filled Braedon's heart with strength, courage, and determination, preparing him for what lay ahead.

15

PROMETHEUS

"General Prometheus, I…we are honored to assist you!"

The seven-foot tall, muscular form turned to face the speaker. Upon spying the Dehali military general, the genetically and technologically-enhanced Guardian leader smiled in satisfaction at the look of revulsion and fear he saw reflected in the eyes of the man.

Thanks to the wizardry of the Elysium scientists, Prometheus had been genetically altered before birth. They had imbued his developing embryo and several other embryos with specific traits from half a dozen of the most powerful animals they could get their hands on, particularly those of the vicious reptilian *sviths*.

The gene-splicing was most prominently seen on the man's face. Although his features were predominantly human, the *svith* DNA had elongated his nose and filled his snout with razor-like teeth. Twin, twisted horns adorned his forehead and broke through the blood-red scales that covered his skin. Even though the horns were not as long as those on a true *svith*, they were still several inches in length and hung over his brow, as if waiting to impale some foe.

Beginning at the crown of his head and running down his spine were metal-capped ridges.

As a counterpoint to his genetic mixing, the scientists had also made several technological "improvements" to his body. His solid black armor covered the scars from his numerous muscle enhancements, but the implant on his face was obtrusive and blatant. A semicircular attachment with barbs piercing down into the scales surrounded his yellowish left eye like the claw of some bird of prey.

The would-be gods in Elysium had created their masterpiece, and his image truly reflected the vileness of his makers. But in the process of his development, the scientists made numerous mistakes developing the chimeras. Unfortunately for the majority of Prometheus's brothers and sisters, the blending of the genetic material usually produced grotesque mutations that were unsuitable for life, much less superior intelligence.

Then again, sometimes, in the darkness and despair of his own mind, Prometheus wondered if perhaps *they* were the fortunate ones. His life had been one of pain and brutality…and service. Although the price he had to pay for each new technological enhancement would be considered by many to be torture, to him, it was worth it. With each new implant came more control—more power.

At least that's what he thought at first, until he discovered the truth.

The chains of his slavery ran deep. He loathed Mathison, but he respected his shrewdness. The governor of Elysium and his cronies knew that in order to keep their "Guardians" in line, they had to have leverage. And that leverage came in the form of a special implant connected to each of their hearts. If Prometheus, or any of the other Guardians, stepped out of line, those who controlled the devices had to simply enter the right code, and the heart would stop.

And with the Pandora's Box implants, entering that code was as quick and easy as formulating a thought. Someday, he hoped to find a way to escape from this life of slavery and become the master. But until then, he would be forced to be Mathison's lackey.

As such, he was required to put up with fools like the puny, Hindu general standing before him. "General Ranjit," Prometheus stated, returning his focus to the present, "thank you for your cooperation."

"Of course," Ranjit stated as he looked directly at the Guardian.

Although Prometheus normally found the company of unaltered humans intolerable, he suddenly began changing his initial assessment of this one. When facing the Titan in full, jet-black Guardian armor, most men either shook with abject terror, or averted their gaze to look anywhere but at him. The Dehali general, on the other hand, actually had the nerve to return his gaze. Prometheus smiled despite himself.

"On behalf of the government of Dehali, we welcome you to our great city," Ranjit said in his best diplomatic tone. "We are ready to offer you and the Elysium Security Force whatever assistance is necessary to help apprehend the fugitives. Our facilities are at your disposal," he stated as he made a sweeping gesture toward the window on the far side of the room in which they stood. On the other side of the glass, technicians, computer programmers, and military commanders were going about their various tasks, oblivious to the presence of their "guests,"

Although Prometheus turned toward the window, his silence left his host guessing as to his thoughts. Deciding to simply continue with his message, he continued. "Governor Khatri and the Ruling Council of Dehali have given me full authority in this matter. They wish for me to express to you that it is our privilege to aid one of this territory's oldest allies."

It took a supreme effort for Prometheus to hide his sneer at the man's words. He knew enough of politics to know that Dehali recognized that Elysium had a distinct military advantage, and so their spineless leaders would naturally bend over backward to appease Mathison. Then again, based on the reports he'd received from several of his men, that advantage may not last as long as Mathison believed.

On their way into this facility, Prometheus had spotted several new heavily-armored combat droids manning the perimeter. While Mathison's researchers were focused on biological engineering, Khatri's techs were focused on mechanical engineering. If it came to war, Prometheus wondered which side would come out on top. Although he and his Guardians were stronger and faster, they were fewer in number. If these new droids proved as powerful as they appeared, Elysium's elite soldiers would be hard-pressed to take them down.

"Indeed," Prometheus replied, his distaste for politics was even worse than his distaste for average humans. "This operation won't take long. The ESF operatives that tracked the fugitives to the city have provided us with several leads."

"I understand," Ranjit replied simply.

However, the two short words caught the Titan's attention. Something in the man's mannerisms gave Prometheus the odd feeling that he was holding something back. But before he could dwell on it further, one of his men entered the room, breaking into his musings.

"Sir?"

Prometheus turned to face the other. "Yes, Cerberus?"

A Type II Guardian, Cerberus was genetically altered but contained very little in the way of technological enhancements. However, what he lacked in hardware he made up for in animalistic instincts, speed, and strength. As he spoke, his canine features twitched in irritation. "Sir, our investigation at the Om Hotel has turned up empty. Based on the DNA testing on the items we found in a bathroom, we know that it was the con artist Xavier who impersonated the scientist and retrieved the message. But even with the help of the hotel staff, we were unable to obtain a copy of the original message from their memory banks. The encryption erased all trace of it after it was retrieved."

"What about the scientist's friend, Travis? Any sign of he or his family?" the Guardian leader asked.

Cerberus hesitated for a moment, his gaze shifting nervously. "We…we tracked down his home, but…but it appears to have been recently abandoned. His family has also disappeared."

Prometheus swore. "Have the ESF continue their search and surveillance. I want every known family member, contact, and acquaintance under direct observation, and I want our men monitoring all transmitted messages, files, financial records—everything! General Ranjit," he said, returning his attention to the other man, "it appears that we could use your help after all."

"We are at your service."

A sneer of frustration curled Prometheus's reptilian lip. Thus far, these lowlife criminals had been careful to cover their tracks and stay one step ahead of his team. But he knew that wouldn't last long. Eventually they would get desperate or sloppy. One of them would slip up, and when they did, he would descend upon them like a predator upon its prey.

"General?"

Ranjit looked up from the datapad he'd been reading to see his lieutenant approaching, his expression one of deep concern. "Yes, what is it?" Ranjit replied, forcing the weariness out of his voice.

Before speaking, the lieutenant's gaze shifted nervously around the area. To Ranjit, it appeared as if the man feared a specter or ghost was going to suddenly pounce on him from the shadows. Then again, considering that these abominations that Mathison called Guardians were still standing less than one hundred feet away on the other side of the main control room, he well understood the man's fear. "I...do you...I mean..."

Ranjit, sensing the man's discomfiture and its probable source, held up a hand, quickly stopping the man's words before they could form a coherent sentence. Opening up a connection to the man through his implant, Ranjit offered a terse warning. *Do not speak. If our intel is correct, these Guardian's have enhanced hearing. Despite the noise and size of this room, I don't want us to take any chances. Now, what is it?*

Nodding in acknowledgement of his superior's command, the man responded. *Many of the men are...uncomfortable with these...with us helping the Guardians. Surely the council...*

Ranjit frowned. *Yes, I understand their misgivings. However, Governor Khatri and the Council has ordered that we assist in any way. Those are your orders, Lieutenant.* Snapping to attention, the other saluted. "Yes, sir!" he said aloud. Without another word, he turned on his heel and headed off toward where Prometheus and three other Guardians stood studying a holographic image. Although Ranjit's eyes tracked the man's movements for several more seconds, his mind was focused on his own misgivings.

Governor Khatri had to maintain positive relations with Elysium. However, if Sarbjeet's information was reliable—and his information was *always* reliable—than Mathison was preparing to make an enormous power grab that would affect all of Tartarus. And with Dehali as his closest neighbor, its citizens would likely bear the brunt of the first assault. Ranjit was determined to make sure that didn't happen.

Upon learning that the Guardians would be arriving, he had given orders to have several of the recent LKT-57 combat droids placed on duty. Perhaps when Mathison received word of Dehali's newest defensive weapons, he would delay his attack long enough for at least the first wave of the new *Jagannath* hovertanks to roll off of the assembly line. Maybe, with this information from Sarbjeet, he could convince Khatri and the council to approve a preemptive strike against Elysium.

Either way, it was time to act. Although he and his men loathed the very presence of these monstrosities, perhaps he could use their being here to his advantage…

Smiling as his idea took shape, Ranjit glanced across the room at the Guardian leader. With or without the council's approval, he would find a way to strike the first blow.

16

UNDERCOVER

Moments after the vehicle pulled into the parking spot, the engine shut down and its doors opened. Four men of Indian descent exited and moved toward the trunk area. Two of the men opened the trunk and began retrieving a pair of large, black equipment bags while the other two carefully scanned the parking garage for any signs that they were being observed.

Each of the bags was three feet long, just over a foot wide, and extremely heavy. Fortunately for their owners, the cumbersome objects had been fitted with repulsors, allowing them to be pushed gently forward on soft cushions of air. Once the bags were clear of the vehicle, the men closed the trunk and began walking toward the building on the other side of the street.

We're approaching the Welcome Center. Are you guys ready to bail us out if this goes bad?

I'm offended at your lack of faith in my false IDs, Braedon, Kianna replied through the implant connection translator. Although she didn't have the technological enhancement herself, the translator allowed her to communicate with those who did. *Those guards at the entrance probably haven't had anything more exciting happen in the past ten years than a drunk guy passing out on the doorstep. If I was a betting lady, I'd put a wager on them giving barely more than a yawn to four boring scientists showing up to take readings on the portal. I think I'd be more worried about Xavier's holographic disguises blowing your cover.*

Hey, now, Xavier's voice cut in, *as long as none of us sticks his head in the Fountain of Shiva, we shouldn't have a problem. My biggest complaint about this whole plan has to do with us waiting around for who-knows-how-long before the portal actually opens.*

It could be worse, Kianna replied, her voice playful. *You could be stuck back here in the Spelunker with Old Sourpuss, like me. Man, does that guy ever smile?*

Braedon fought to suppress a laugh. *Only when he's making others miserable.*

Well, I sure hope that portal opens up pretty soon, Kianna replied. *I know you guys need me back here in case I need to hack into something, but I'd much rather have come along. The rate things are going, Charon's gonna be smiling a **lot** from the amount of misery he's causing me! Just get those readings and get back here as soon as you can.*

We'll do our best, Braedon stated. *Let's just pray that Gunther's guess is correct about the next portal opening. Otherwise, we could be here for a while.*

Okay, you two. Cut the chatter. Xavier said as he turned to glance at Braedon who was walking beside him, the holographic mask making the soldier appear to be a middle-aged Indian man with a thick mustache. *We're here. Time for the "master" to perform his magic!* Shutting down the connection, he turned to give the two men behind him a quick glance. "Gunther, Travis…just relax and follow my lead."

Taking a deep breath, Xavier, in the guise of a Hindu man in his late fifties, led the small party through the doors of the Dehali Welcome Center and strode up to the security counter. Doing his best to ignore the sight of a pair of four-foot SK-200 security droids resting on the floor against the wall on each side of the foyer, he cleared his throat and addressed the two guards standing behind the counter. "Hi. I'm Professor Nayar from the Dehali Science Academy. My colleagues and I are here to take some readings on the portal. You should have been notified of our arrival. Our work is quite important. In fact, we're hoping that with the data we collect, we'll be able to—"

The security guard on the left stood to his feet and quickly cut off Xavier, probably in the hopes of being spared a lengthy, scientific lecture. "What's in the bags?"

Xavier paused for a moment before answering, as if he was trying to decide whether or not to be offended at the interruption. "That's our surveying equipment."

"Put it over there," the man said, pointing toward a sensor table off to his right. The inflection in the man's voice left no doubt in Xavier's mind that he found this aspect of his job tedious, which was exactly what Xavier had been hoping for.

While the attention of the guards was fixed upon Travis and Gunther, who were moving the bags toward the scanner, Braedon sent a wireless message through his implant, releasing the robotic hacking device hidden in the sole of his left shoe. Immediately, the miniscule robot, which resembled a tiny needle, hovered under the desk until it arrived at its destination. Attaching itself to the bottom of the desk, it began its task of infiltrating the Welcome Center's computer system. Within moments, Braedon and Xavier heard the confirmation from Kianna through their implants. *Got it! I'll have only limited access until the Leech finishes its job, but don't worry. I shouldn't have any problem making sure you guys are cleared.*

With the device in place, Braedon casually strode over to where the guard was examining the equipment. Assessing the situation with a trained eye, he felt his pulse quicken. As a soldier, he had been in many situations that required him to suppress and hide his emotions and feelings. Xavier, with his training as an actor and his experience as a con man, looked completely natural and relaxed.

Gunther and Travis, however, looked nervous and on the verge of losing their composure. And based on the suspicious glare being sent toward the two from the guard on Braedon's left, he knew they were in real danger of discovery.

"Dr. Dubashi," Xavier said calmly to the holographically disguised Travis as he placed a hand on his shoulder, "are you okay?"

For a second, Braedon couldn't believe that Xavier would draw attention to the man's obvious nervousness. But then, to his surprise, Braedon could see that Xavier, whose back was turned to the guards, was sending a quick teleconnect message to Travis.

Sure enough, Travis replied a moment later, his voice shaky. "I…I'm just…worried about the possibility that we…we won't have the equipment in place by the time the next portal opens."

Not missing a beat, Xavier furrowed his brow with concern. "I know. But there's nothing we can do about that right now. I told you there would likely be delays. The best we can do is be patient and hope we have enough time to set up once we're through. For now, why don't you and Dr. Trivedi," he said, glancing at Gunther, "give the guard your thumbprints so they can get us cleared?"

Nodding, Travis and Gunther left the equipment scanning station and walked back toward the main security desk. As they did so, Braedon let out a small sigh as the expression on the guard's face lost most of its suspicion. Looking over at Xavier, Braedon caught the slightest hint of relief on the con man's face before he turned back to where the guard stood examining the equipment.

With one crisis averted, Braedon returned his focus to the guard running the computer. If Kianna didn't get their thumbprints, pictures, and other information into the system, then nothing else mattered. Doing his best to remain calm, Braedon watched the guard's face intently as the man studied his display screen.

Kianna, what's going on? Braedon said through the implant connection. *We need that clearance **now***!

A second later, Kianna's reply came through, her words tense and clipped. *I'm having some…trouble…getting their stupid system to let me in! I didn't expect a simple Welcome Center to have so much encryption! These guys really—*

Braedon missed the rest of her sentence as his attention was brought abruptly back to his current situation. He felt his stomach tighten as the guard frowned. "Dr. Dubashi, it seems that the system couldn't find your information. Could you please place your thumb on the reader once again?" After casting a nervous glance at Gunther, Travis did as instructed.

Taking a casual step forward, Braedon positioned himself near the guard. As he did so, he noticed that Xavier had also moved closer to the other guard performing the scan on their equipment. If necessary, Braedon believed they could easily take out the two men, but the SK-200 security droids would be another matter entirely.

Although somewhat smaller than the SK-290 security droids that Sarbjeet had positioned outside his mansion, the SK-200 models retained the same basic look as their larger cousins, including the human-shaped torso, dark-blue visors, and impressive weaponry. Their overall smaller size meant that they were quicker and more maneuverable inside a building. If it came to a fight with the droids, Braedon knew they would likely end up as prisoners.

C'mon, Kianna! We need that clearance now!

Maybe I'd have it quicker if you'd just shut up and let me…wait…wait…I got it! she replied in triumph.

Suddenly, the guard's expression changed. "There it is. Sorry about the wait, Doctor. We've been having a few technical issues lately."

Clearly relieved, Travis stepped aside to allow Gunther to access the print reader.

Thanks, Kianna, Braedon said through the connection. *It appears your reputation will remain intact after all.*

Ha! As if there was ever any doubt. Despite her bravado, Braedon could still detect traces of tension in her voice. *Now get moving.*

Closing down the connection, Braedon settled in to wait. Fortunately, he didn't have to wait long. Within less than five minutes, the guards had finished their inspection of the equipment, and the four of them were cleared. Using their newly acquired security badges, Braedon and the others passed through the main doors and headed toward the interior of the Welcome Center.

"Well, that was fun," Xavier whispered as they strode down the main hallway. "Gunther, if we make it through this, remind me to give you and Travis some acting pointers. You two looked about as nervous as long-tailed cats in a room full of rocking chairs!"

Embarrassed, the two men didn't reply but simply continued walking down the hall while pushing the hovering bags of equipment. The Dehali Welcome Center appeared much like the one in Elysium. It was designed to be warm and inviting, with numerous statues, paintings, and sculptures lining the walls and filling alcoves. Plants and flowers accentuated the warm red and gold paint on the walls.

Based on the schematics that Kianna had provided, Braedon knew that the central hallway of the structure led to a section of the building that was shaped like a wedge. The tip of the wedge consisted of the main room that surrounded the area where the portals typically appeared. The rest of the building housed numerous rooms where the new arrivals were taken for processing.

As they walked, Braedon thought back on his own arrival in Tartarus. Although it happened ten years ago, the familiar sights and sounds of this facility brought the memories back in a rush. He still remembered the confusion and disorientation vividly. Like many, he had to be sedated more than once before he was able to function enough to understand what the Welcome Center workers were explaining to him. The initial shock had left him numb. Then, slowly, the truth began to work its way into his petrified mind. With the truth came anger, fear, depression, and nightmares.

It took him years to get over it all. He could still remember the dreams of his wife, screaming and reaching out to him as he plunged into darkness….

"Professor Nayar, I presume."

The voice intruded upon Braedon's dark thoughts, bringing him back to the present. Thankful for the interruption, he turned his full attention to the speaker. A balding Hindu man with thick glasses and dressed in a white, medical coat strode up to greet Xavier with an outstretched hand.

Falling naturally into character, Xavier returned the greeting. "Dr. Rana," he said, recognizing the man from profile pictures Kianna had given them, "thank you for this opportunity. The academy board is very grateful."

Dr. Rana nodded. "We're glad to help. I only wish that we had been informed of your visit much sooner. Somehow, your initial request didn't get forwarded to us."

Xavier frowned. "Really? That's odd. I was informed by the board that the request had been submitted and approved months ago by Director Ganaka."

"Indeed, that seems to be the case," Dr. Rana replied. "Once I heard you had arrived, I searched back through the records and discovered the request. I apologize for any inconvenience this may have caused you. Rest assured that we'll do everything necessary to offer our assistance."

"Thank you, Dr. Rana," Xavier said, bowing slightly.

"If you follow me, I'll lead you to the Portal room so you can set up your equipment," the doctor stated as he headed off down the hall at a brisk pace. "There has been no portal activity for several weeks, so we're expecting one to appear at any time. I'm sure you're anxious to get set up. It would be very unfortunate if you missed your window of opportunity."

"Yes, it would," Xavier replied with an extra edge to his voice. "Thank you for understanding our impatience."

Offering a quick nod, Dr. Rana continued. "Once your equipment is in place, I'll show you where you can store your personal belongings and where you can sleep, if that becomes necessary. Hopefully, the portal will appear quickly so you can get back to your research. I do hope you'll share your findings with us once everything is complete."

"Absolutely!" Xavier said. Lowering his voice, he leaned in toward Dr. Rana, a conspiratorial tone to his voice. "Actually, we hope to do more than that. Although the academy board has urged me not to reveal this to anyone, I believe they would understand if I share it with you, since you are directly involved. However, I need your word that you won't disclose this information to anyone."

Dr. Rana slowed his walk, an air of importance crossing his features. "Yes, of course. I understand the importance of matters such as these."

"Excellent," Xavier stated. "I appreciate your discretion. As I was saying, we hope that once our research is finalized, we will be able to use the data to create portals of our own that can be controlled. If we're correct, we will be able to use these portals to cross from one end of the galaxy to another, including returning to Earth!"

Shock and awe filled the man, causing him to stop in his tracks. "That is…that's incredible! This could mean…this would change everything!"

"Exactly," Xavier confirmed as he gently prodded the man to continue walking. "Which is why it is imperative that the academy keeps this project secret. If word were to get out before the research is complete…"

"Yes, I understand," Dr. Rana said numbly, his mind still reeling from the news. "Here we are now," he said as the group approached a set of double doors. "Let's get you set up quickly!"

Opening the doors, the Welcome Center's head medical technician led his visitors into a large room that was, like the building as a whole, shaped like a wedge, or a quarter circle. In addition to the central entrance, there were two more entrances—one on the left corner and one on the right corner of the wedge. The design reminded Braedon of some kind of theater. Although the room was over one hundred feet wide at its widest point and over one hundred and fifty feet long, it remained almost completely empty. However, what it lacked in furniture, it made up for in beauty and artistry. Much like the rest of the Welcome Center, it was lined with intricate patterns and colorful flourishes that were designed to put the viewer at ease.

However, despite the beauty along the walls, scuff marks and discolorations on the floor tiles evidenced the locations of past portal appearances and reminded Braedon of the tragedies that unfolded in this place. After a quick, cursory count, he identified six different scuff-marked areas, with the most prominent being at the center of the room.

"You should have almost complete privacy here," Dr. Rana said hurriedly as Gunther, Travis, and Braedon began unloading the bags and setting up the equipment. "That is, of course, until a portal opens. When that happens, my staff will enter from each of the three main entrances. Since we don't know exactly where the portal will appear, I would suggest setting up along the walls. Will that be a problem?"

Xavier glanced at Gunther and Travis for confirmation before replying. "No. All of our equipment will be placed on hovering platforms, allowing us to move close enough to get the readings when the time comes."

"Good. If you have need of anything else, just teleconnect me," he said as he handed Xavier his direct dial code. "I'll leave you to set up. Again, just let me know if you need anything else. I'll inform my staff not to disturb you."

Grabbing his hand, Xavier shook it emphatically. "Thank you, Dr. Rana, for your hospitality and your understanding."

"You're welcome. Who knows, perhaps we'll all be in the history records some day for the parts we played!" he stated.

"Who knows?" Xavier echoed as Dr. Rana exited the room.

"Nicely done," Braedon quipped once they were alone. "I see now why you were able to make a living at acting for awhile. Why did you ever quit?"

Xavier turned to regard Braedon, his holographic expression giving Braedon no hints as to what the man was feeling. "I got tired of it. My fame made me a prisoner. I couldn't walk around in public without people recognizing me. That's one of the reasons I began investing in these holographic masks."

"Well, it's certainly proved useful," Braedon said. Letting the conversation drop, he opened a connection through his implant. *Kianna, we're in position. It should only take us a couple of minutes to get everything set.*

Thank God, she replied. *Now let's just hope that portal opens up before anyone decides to check on your story. The idea of all of those Guardians snooping around the city makes me just a wee bit uneasy.*

Yeah, no kidding, Braedon agreed. *I don't know what Raptor and Jade have cooked up, but I hope it'll keep them occupied long enough for us to collect the data and get out of the city.*

There was a short pause before Kianna's voice returned. *Now that you guys are set, I'm gonna go get some food, okay? I need a break. Keep me posted.*

Okay. Watch yourself, Braedon said then closed down the connection. Although he busied himself with helping the others set up the equipment, his thoughts were still dwelling on his conversation with Kianna. What exactly *did* Raptor and Jade have in mind? He knew it was something that was supposed to keep the Guardians, the ESF and local Dehali police occupied, but he didn't like the fact that Raptor hadn't let him in on the secret. Whatever it was, he just hoped it worked. Otherwise, things might get very unpleasant for all of them…

17

THE PORTAL OPENS

Kianna was rudely awakened by the sound of Charon swearing harshly. Startled, she sat bolt upright in one of the rear seats of the Spelunker where she had been lounging.

"We've got company," he said irritably as he pointed to the holographic screen that hovered before him.

Shaking off her slumber, Kianna focused on the image and inhaled sharply. A pair of Type I, technologically-enhanced Guardians were stepping out of a large transport along with a contingent of six Dehali military troops. The Cyborgs were dressed in full, black Guardian armor with helmets that obscured their faces. Although they appeared unarmed, Kianna knew that they contained several types of weapons within the casings of their armor. The military troops, however, clearly had pistols riding in holsters on their hips.

"Why are they here? I don't see any indication that Braedon and the others were discovered."

"Raptor thought this might happen. That's why he prepared a diversion," Charon said. "He guessed that since the ESF know the Vortex is related to the portals that they might keep an eye on the Welcome Center. Best case scenario, they're here on a routine visit. Worst case—someone inside ratted us out."

Glancing out the window toward the ceiling of the cavern, Kianna noted that the threads of light that laced the rock walls around the city and served to regulate sleep cycles was set to one of its dimmest settings. "It's still fairly early in the morning."

"That doesn't tell us much," Charon replied. "Sometimes these military types like to get a jump on things in the morning to catch people off guard and half asleep. I'll contact Raptor and tell him to start his diversion. You call the others and tell them to get out of there."

"Right," Kianna agreed as she switched seats in order to be closer to the computer control panel that was located just behind the driver's chair.

"Braedon. Xavier," she said, speaking into the implant translator. "Stay alert. You boys've got a pair of Cyborgs entering the building along with six friends from the Dehali military. Charon's gonna have Raptor begin his diversion. Pray that it works. Otherwise you're gonna have to get out of there mighty quick!"

I was afraid of this. I really thought this was going to work. Braedon was silent for several seconds as he waged an internal war against his own frustration. *We'll be ready. I'll wake the others and tell them—*

He stopped so abruptly that, for a moment, Kianna thought she had somehow lost the connection with him. However, he returned a moment later, his voice filled with excitement. *An alarm is going off throughout the building! A portal is opening. If Raptor's diversion doesn't work, see if you can stall them. I've gotta go!*

Stunned, Kianna sat there for a moment and let his words sink in. "'Stall them'?" she said aloud to herself. "And just how am I supposed to do that?"

"What's wrong?" Charon said as he closed down his own implant connection with Raptor and returned his focus back to her.

"The portal's beginning to open!" she said without even looking at him. Flipping on the computer's holographic screen, she began working furiously. "If the diversion doesn't work, Braedon wants us to try stalling the Cyborgs until Travis and Gunther finish getting their readings."

"Did he say how long that would take?" the burly man asked irritably.

"No. I'm not even sure he knows."

"Well, that's just great," Charon spat sarcastically. "I can tell you one thing, I ain't dying for this stupid mission. If Raptor feels so strongly about it, he can do it himself. I'm sitting this one out." Having finished his monologue, he leaned back in his chair, placed his hands behind his head, and closed his eyes, as if preparing to take a nap.

Kianna narrowed her eyes at him in disgust. "But what about the others? Don't you even care what happens to your friends?"

Opening his eyes, he calmly returned her gaze. "Look, lady. Soldier boy and his scientist buddies aren't my friends. In fact, I've been telling Raptor all along that we're wasting our time. As far as I'm concerned, let them get caught. The only reason Raptor's even got me sitting out here is to make sure that *if they succeed*, they uphold their end of the bargain and don't run off on us."

"Wow, your sentiment just fills me up with warm fuzzies," she quipped sarcastically. "What about Xavier? I thought he was part of your little gang."

Charon shrugged. "I've got no love for him. He's ticked me off more times than I can count. I tolerate him because he's useful. But I frankly couldn't care less about him."

Kianna's lip curled. "You certainly live up to your reputation as a mercenary." Turning away, she focused on her computer screen. However, sudden movement coming from the main entrance of the Welcome Center caught her attention. Grabbing her teleconnect translator, she dialed up Braedon's direct line in excitement. "Braedon, it seems that whatever Raptor did, it certainly helped. One of the Cyborgs and all the Dehali soldiers are leaving the Welcome Center. From the looks of it, they're in quite a hurry."

That's great! Braedon replied. *What about the other Guardian?*

Kianna frantically scanned the hacked camera feeds from inside the building. "He's in the main hallway heading right toward you."

We've gotta slow him down! Cyborg enhancements allow them to see through holograms. If he reaches us, our cover'll be blown. Do you have access to building controls? Can you lock the doors to the portal room?

"Yeah," she said, her fingers flying over the controls on the holographic screen. "It should only take me a minute. But that won't hold him for long."

Forget it, Braedon said rapidly. *If you lock the doors, Dr. Rana will know we've hacked their system. Just be ready for anything! I've got a better idea!*

The connection ended abruptly. "It better be a good one," Kianna mumbled to herself. "God help them!"

"Dr. Rana!" Braedon called across the room as he rushed toward the man. Surrounded by his team of a dozen medical technicians and their hovering gurneys and supplies, Braedon had to work his way through the group to reach the doctor.

Upon seeing the intense expression on the face of one of his visitors, Dr. Rana stiffened in alarm. "What is it? What's wrong?"

"We're in serious danger! We need you to lock the doors immediately!"

"Wha—why? What's going on?" the doctor replied in confusion.

"I'll explain in a moment. But please, lock the doors now!" Braedon urged.

Nodding, Dr. Rana's eyes flattened as he relayed a message through his implant. Once completed, his attention returned to Braedon. "Done. Now explain, and do it quickly. The portal is almost open and I need to direct my team. As soon as that happens, I'll have to unlock the doors so we can treat the incoming patients."

Wasting no time, Braedon spoke, the words tumbling out of his mouth in a mad rush. "I just received word that a Guardian from Elysium is here! Governor Mathison has secretly been trying to get hold of our research for years! The Guardian will kill everyone in this facility to get to us, if necessary!

The blood drained out of Dr. Rana's face, leaving him pale and ghostly in the shimmering purplish light from the forming portal. "But...but to attack a Guardian could... could cause serious problems between the governments of Elysium and Dehali! I can't…I can't make that kind of decision!"

"You don't have to attack it," Braedon stated quickly. "Just have your men divert it long enough for us to finish our readings and get out."

Dr. Rana considered the suggestion for a moment then nodded his assent. "Okay. I'll give the word."

Braedon heaved a sigh of relief. "Thank you." Placing a hand on the man's shoulder in gratitude, Braedon turned away and headed back toward Gunther, Travis, and Xavier, who all waited nervously for news. However, before he could update the others on the situation, a final swooshing sound filled the room, signaling the opening of the portal.

"Um…excuse me, Master Guardian," the white-robed Welcome Center technician stated as he raised a hand to garner the attention of the six-foot, four-inch Cyborg. Without breaking stride, the technologically-enhanced man turned his helmeted head to peer at one of his three guides who walked beside him. "Yes, what is it?"

The sound of the electronically-filtered voice caused the man to tremble and sputter. "I…I… Sir, if you please…Dr. Rana would…would like us to…. A portal has just opened, and we will be receiving new arrivals within moments. He asks that…he requests that you hold off your…your inspection until they have been…until they have been treated. Then he will show you around the facilities personally."

The Guardian came to an abrupt halt, causing two of his escorts to nearly stumble into each other. "Inform Dr. Rana that in compliance with article 3, section II of the recent cooperative agreement between Governor Mathison and Governor Khatri, I have been granted full access to this facility. I would like to see the portal for myself!"

Without waiting for their response, the Guardian began walking toward the double doors at the end of the hallway that led to the Portal Room.

Casting a quick glance at his colleagues, the panicked technician moved to catch up to the figure. "But, sir, Dr. Rana is happy to comply with the agreement. However, he...he requests that you not interrupt during this...this delicate time of welcoming our new citizens and...and he hopes you will not deny him the honor of showing you about personally. Please!"

Ignoring the man, the Guardian strode up to the doors and nearly ran into them as they failed to open. Slowly, the black mask that obscured his face turned to face the technician, who backed into the wall behind him. "What is the meaning of this?" the Guardian said, the electronics in the helmet only adding to the icy tone of his voice.

"I...I assure you I...I don't know!" he stammered as he desperately looked across the hall at his colleagues for support. However, both of them were terror-stricken and had begun backing slowly down the hall, their eyes fixed upon the Guardian.

"I demand to see Dr. Rana *now!*" the Cyborg said, his voice rising ominously as he moved toward the unfortunate technician, who was sliding down the wall into a crumpled heap on the floor.

The sound of booted feet approaching diverted the Guardian's attention. Coming down the hall were the two guards stationed at the security desk, their hands resting on the handles of their holstered weapons. Behind them glided the two KL-12 Security droids, their armored bodies floating noiselessly over the tile floor.

At the sight of the guards and their robotic counterparts, the Cyborg straightened to his full height, his stance wary. "I demand access to this room. If you do not comply, I will consider this act a violation of the agreement between Elysium and Dehali. Open the doors."

Swallowing nervously, the older of the two guards spoke. "I'm sorry, Master Guardian, but we have orders to direct you to one of our guest suites until such time as Dr. Rana can attend to you himself."

The Cyborg cocked his head at a slight angle as the three technicians turned and fled down the hall. "And if I refuse?" he challenged. "Are you really willing to go against the wishes of your government over something so trivial, or are you hiding something?"

The guards looked at each other, their faces full of doubt and confusion.

In that moment of indecision, the Guardian struck.

Raising his right arm with enhanced speed, the Cyborg launched a concentrated EMP pulse from a hidden compartment on the back of his hand toward the Sentry droid on the right. The bolt of electromagnetic energy struck the droid in its torso. Immediately upon impact, sparks of electricity arched all around it, causing its servos and actuators to twitch and spasm. Even before the droid's anti-gravity repulsors gave out and dropped the machine to the floor, the Guardian dove forward into a roll to avoid the retaliatory barrage of laser fire from the remaining Sentry.

Slower to respond, the guard directly in front of the downed droid tried to draw his blaster but was knocked backward before he could complete the movement by a well-placed kick from the Cyborg.

Crouching low, the Guardian turned to face the second guard who now stood directly between the other Sentry and its target. Unable to get a clear shot on the attacker, the Sentry droid glided sideways across the width of the hallway.

Meanwhile, the other guard had pulled out his weapon and began firing wildly at the Cyborg. Several of his shots glanced off the Guardian's black armor but failed to slow him down. Letting out an angry, desperate yell, the guard moved backward down the hall even as the armored figure leapt from his crouched position and tackled the man to the floor.

Using the terrified man's body as a shield, the Guardian rolled over just as the Sentry droid opened fire. Immediately, the guard grunted in pain, his body going limp. Gathering his strength, the prone Cyborg used his enhanced arm muscles to launch the unconscious man's body toward the droid. Even before it collided with the robot, the Guardian was back on his feet.

The collision with the guard gave the Cyborg just enough time to close the distance between himself and the Sentry. As the droid released a new barrage of laser fire, the Guardian unleashed an attack with his compression pistol located on his left wrist. Based on the same anti-gravity technology that allowed the robot to stay afloat, the weapon sent a wall of force toward an opponent. The invisible attack swiveled the droid's torso, causing its laser to go wide.

Taking advantage of the respite, the Guardian dove forward and grabbed the Sentry's left arm. With the aid of his technologically enhanced muscles, he ripped the appendage off of the robot. Ignoring the fluid and oil that sprayed out from the damaged machine, the technologically-enhanced human used the metal arm as a club to knock out the droid's main sensor display, effectively blinding it. Stepping quickly back from the flailing Sentry, the Guardian quickly fired an EMP blast into its chest, ending the battle.

With his foes defeated, the Cyborg turned back towards his original objective. As he took his first step toward the doors leading into the Portal Room, he realized that his armor had failed to stop two of the Sentry's blasts: one in his right leg, the other in his right side. Limping up to the doors, he considered whether or not to update Prometheus on the situation. Making up his mind, the Guardian prepared a short message that would be relayed in the unlikely event of his death.

He would contact Prometheus, but not before he found out exactly what or who was hiding behind these doors.

18

THE DIVERSION

"Xavier and the others have some unwelcome company," Raptor said to Jade, who sat next to him in the driver's seat of the Obsidian. "It looks like break time's over."

"Good," Jade replied as she opened her almond-shaped eyes and brushed a lock of loose, jet-black hair out of her face. "I've had my share of down time. It seems that all we've been doing for the past week and a half since arriving is running errands and waiting." Firing up the engine of the sleek, black hovercar, she flipped the switch to deactivate the computer driver, put the car into gear, and pulled out onto the mostly deserted street. "I'm telling you, Raptor, if this thing doesn't work, I'm ready to call it quits on this whole thing."

"Yeah, well, it might be too late for that," Raptor said. It had been eighteen days since he'd first been given the prophecy by Steven, and most of the urgency he'd felt had since worn off. However, even without the immediate threat of his impending demise to drive him, there were still other factors to consider. "Even if this doesn't pan out, we still can't just sit back and let Mathison and his Guardians make mindless drones out of everyone in Tartarus. It's bad for business."

Jade cast him a lopsided grin in response to his jest. Next to her on the seat, Zei, her pet *mindim*, chirped softly as it stared up at her with its wide, rodent-like eyes. Reaching over, she stroked the creature's gray fur absentmindedly.

"Not to mention," he continued, "it seems that Tartarus itself might not be around for much longer, what with all of the earthquakes and stuff going on."

At the mention of the quake, Jade's demeanor lost all sense of jollity. "I spoke to Tara last night. She said that Serena was hurt in the earthquake. Rahib, I need to go see my sisters in New China. They need me. I know that what we're doing here is important, but I don't know how much longer I can wait."

Sobered at the emotion exhibited by the normally stoic woman, and the fact that she didn't use his code name, Raptor nodded. "I understand, Mingyu," he said, using her real name in return.

Brushing aside her feelings, Jade slowed the car down and pulled over against the curb, her emotionless mask once again in place. "Let's get this over with."

"Yeah," Raptor said simply. Tapping the door control, he exited the moment it had finished opening. As he strode up to the nearby building, he heard the soft click as the door shut behind him.

Because it was early in the morning, most of the stores were still closed. However, many of the restaurants were already open, as were the temples, which never closed. Here in the second tier of the city, named after the *Vaishya* caste of laborers and merchants, business was going on as usual.

And where there were businesses, there were those in need of credit sticks. Although many governments had tried over the years to eliminate paper currency, they found that there were always those who needed the flexibility, and anonymity, of cash. To compromise, they developed credit sticks, which could be traded simply *as* cash or could be used to wirelessly transfer credits to business or other vendors. For the common people, this arrangement worked just fine. For the government, it still allowed them to trace transactions from the banks to the stick dispensing machines and, in some cases, even place trackers on sticks purchased from flagged accounts of known criminals and other enemies of the state.

Which was exactly what Raptor was counting on.

Walking up to the machine, he placed his thumb on the reader. Within seconds, the holographic screen appeared, along with the words "WELCOME, GUNTHER LUESCHEN." Raptor let out the breath that he hadn't even realized he had been holding. Although he never had any serious doubt that Xavier's false thumbprint would work, there was always a chance that this time would be the exception. Knowing that even now the Guardians, Elysium Security Forces and Dehali military would be alerted to his activity, he quickly withdrew several hundred credits and ended the transaction. Returning to the Obsidian, he climbed inside, forcing himself to remain calm and relaxed.

"Do you really think they'll take the bait?" Jade asked once he was settled in.

"They'd be fools not to," he replied. "If it was one of us, they'd probably realize it's a setup. But Gunther is just a common citizen. They might think he just grew desperate for credits and risked making a withdrawal, perhaps not even realizing that the military could track them."

Jade cocked her head to the side. "Well, I'm sure we'll find out soon enough. It's too bad we can't add them to our stash."

"I was thinking the same thing. Actually, with the money Braedon got from his Crimson Liberty contacts, we may actually come out ahead on this deal."

Jade shook her head. "If he ever finds out that Sarbjeet actually traded those parts for the information we provided and didn't actually charge us, you'd better watch out. I don't think his friends would be too happy to learn that we didn't really use the money for the parts."

Raptor looked a little defensive. "Hey, but we still used some of it. We did have to pay to rent the Obsidian, buy supplies, and pay Janak and Fulmala. Why should we be the ones to foot the bill for this whole crusade of theirs?"

"I'm not disagreeing with your logic, I'm just saying you'd better be careful."

"Aren't I always?" Raptor replied with a roguish grin.

Smiling, Jade engaged the automatic driving program and focused her attention on looking for any suspicious activity behind them.

They traveled for several more minutes before they finally got the confirmation they had hoped for. "It worked!" Raptor said, his voice containing a contradictory mixture of both relief and anxiety. "Charon said that one of the Guardians and all the Dehali soldiers just left the Welcome Center in a hurry. Wanna place a bet on where they're headed?"

Jade snorted. "No thanks. I like my credits right where they are. Now we just have to hope your little gamble works."

Feigning offense, Raptor cast a hurt look in her direction. "O ye of little faith. It'll work. Everything's gone pretty much according to plan this far."

"Right. Which only means we're overdue for something to go wrong."

"How about putting some confidence in your leader."

Jade didn't respond as the Obsidian drew closer to their destination. They had entered a part of the city that, while not as bad as sections of the lowest level, had clearly seen better days. Business in this district seemed to be struggling to survive. As evidence of that, a rundown office building sat deserted at the end of the street on the corner. The broken windows and filthy facade made it appear to have been abandoned for some time.

But those appearances were wrong.

While they were still half a block away, Jade regained manual control of their vehicle and pulled it into a nearby alley. Bringing the hovercar to a halt, she shut off the engine. Turning toward Raptor, she gave him a quizzical look. "Well? Did any of the toys we left behind detect any movement?"

Raptor studied the readout from his palm-sized holoscreen. "Nothing but a few of Zei's wingless relatives." Shutting down the image, Raptor tucked the device into one of his pockets and pressed the door release.

Once they had exited the vehicle, Raptor and Jade headed down the alley toward the back entrance to the office building. Taking advantage of the opportunity, Zei climbed off of Jade's shoulder, scampered up the side of the nearest building, and leapt into the air, its skin folds keeping it aloft. Reaching the door, Raptor sent a coded signal through his implant to the devices he'd placed inside. A moment later, Jade opened the door, and they stepped inside.

The two moved quickly down the abandoned hallway toward the center of the building, not bothering to turn on any lights. Farther ahead, a pale glow streamed in through the front windows from the ever-increasing veins of light from the cavern ceiling. As they arrived at one of the many doors in the hallway, Raptor stopped. Grabbing the handle, he opened the door as he spoke. "I'll ditch the credit sticks while you—"

He froze instantly, his body becoming rigid and his heart leaping into his throat. Standing inside the room, were six large men, all but one had a weapon pointed at Raptor and Jade. The unarmed man took a step toward them, his face beaming. Taking the tobacco stick out of his mouth, he held out his arms in a welcoming gesture, a wicked grin on his face

"Raptor and Jade, I can't tell you how happy I am to see you! Now, where's that runt brother of mine?"

19

THE PORTAL READINGS

The purple energy from the portal continued to crescendo as the fifteen onlookers watched in silence. Near the back of the large room, Braedon turned toward Gunther and Travis, who were hurriedly tweaking their devices and studying the readouts on the holographic screens. The rest of the occupants of the room consisted of the Welcome Center staff, who awaited the newest arrivals to Tartarus.

Suddenly, a loud bang thundered through the room, causing everyone to jump in surprise. Dr. Rana, who stood several feet away, cast a quick glance at the main entrance before turning his gaze toward Braedon and the others. Moving quickly to join his guests, he spoke, his words coming out jumbled. "The Guardian…he's…he's going to…he's pounding on the door. What happened to the Sentr…what are we going to do?"

Xavier, himself becoming unsettled by the continued pounding, looked nervously at the doctor. "Can you call for more security? There's gotta be more guards somewhere nearby."

Dr. Rana looked confused. "This is a Welcome Center, not a military base! I've already alerted the authorities, but…but it'll take them several minutes to arrive at best!"

At a loss for words, the normally composed Xavier looked toward Braedon, searching for inspiration. "We've got to find a way to slow him down," the soldier replied. "We've got to give Gunther and Travis more time."

The look of confusion on Dr. Rana's face increased. "Who are Gunther and Travis?" he asked.

But before Braedon could think of a way to cover his mistake, the portal opened fully, demanding the attention of everyone in the room. Several seconds later, four figures appeared from within the swirling energy and were dumped unceremoniously onto the floor in a heap. The staff of nurses and technicians immediately leapt into action to assist the four disoriented travelers. Within moments, they had the newcomers sedated and supported by hovering gurneys. Casting their final nervous glances at the main entrance of the room, the groups of workers unlocked the door on the west side of the room. To their great relief, the exit was unobstructed. Moving quickly, they ushered their patients out of the room and into the other areas of the Welcome Center. As the last nurse hurried into the hallway, Dr. Rana slammed the door release to close the door. Once it was closed, he locked it. Turning around, he leaned against it and fought to control his breathing, which was coming in short gasps.

It was only in the silence that followed that Braedon and the others noticed that the pounding on the main entrance had stopped. "Where did it go?" Xavier said, giving voice to the question that was burning in each of their minds.

"I don't know, but I don't want to stick around any longer to find out. Gunther, Travis, did you get the readings?" Braedon asked.

For a moment, neither man spoke as they studied the data they had collected. Finally, after several tense seconds, a slow smile began to spread across Travis's face. "That's it! We got it. This is exactly what we needed."

Letting out a sigh of relief, Braedon breathed a quick prayer. "Great. Now let's get out of here before that Guardian...what? What's wrong?"

Gunther's expression had inexplicably changed from one of triumph to one of deep concern and shock. "No... no this can't be!"

Spreading like a virus, Gunther's sudden change of mood sent a wave of fear through the others. "What 'can't be'?" Xavier echoed.

Staring up at his companions, Gunther had the unmistakable look of one who had just learned a horrible truth. "I...I recognize these numbers. Why...why didn't I see it before? All of those years of research and I...I never saw the truth!"

Grabbing the man's shoulders, Xavier shook him in an effort to bring him back to reality. "What are you talking about? What truth?"

"I know what caused the portals to appear on Earth!"

But before Gunther could elaborate further, a loud crash came from above them. Reflexively, the men threw up their arms to protect themselves as a portion of the ceiling collapsed. Dust and debris clouded the room, choking them and momentarily blinding them.

A black-booted foot kicked out from somewhere within the dust cloud and caught Xavier in the stomach.

The impact sent him flying backward into the nearby wall, where he crumpled to the floor. Dropping into a crouch, the attacker knocked both Travis and Gunther down with a sweep of his foot.

Across the room, Dr. Rana stood in front of the western door as if rooted to the spot, his gaze fixed in horror upon the armored Guardian. Realizing that the doctor was not a threat, the enhanced human turned his full attention toward Braedon, who had just recovered from his initial surprise.

Dropping into a combat stance, Braedon faced the helmeted foe. Although he was over six feet tall, Braedon discovered that he was still several inches shorter than the Guardian. Add to that the man's enhanced strength and speed, and Braedon realized quickly that he had very little chance of defeating his opponent. The last time he had faced one of Elysium's elite guards, he had had Jade's help. Even then, they wouldn't have won had it not been for Gunther's use of the Vortex weapon. Judging by the Guardian's relaxed posture, it seemed he had reached the same conclusion regarding the outcome of the battle.

Praying for help, Braedon leapt forward and attacked. Despite his skill and speed, the larger man easy blocked each jab and kick. After several failed attacks from Braedon, the Guardian counter-attacked, causing his opponent to retreat swiftly to avoid the heavy blows. Each moment that passed left Braedon more battered and bruised until finally his attacker landed a solid blow to the side of the head that sent him reeling.

As Braedon stumbled, the Guardian reached out with his left hand and grabbed him around the neck. Lifting his defeated foe into the air, the Guardian began walking toward the west exit as Braedon struggled to breathe. "Dr. Rana, as a keeper of the peace and friend of the Dehali Council, I regret to inform you that you have been deceived. These men are not what they seem," the Guardian said, his helmet making his voice sound metallic and cold. Reaching up with his gloved right hand, the Guardian released a small shock into Braedon's face, causing him to gasp in pain. Immediately, the holographic mask disappeared, revealing his true features. Dr. Rana brought a hand up to his mouth in surprise.

Finished with his demonstration, the Guardian hurled Braedon across the room to land near Xavier and the others. Turning back to the doctor, he continued. "On behalf of Governor Mathison and the citizens of Elysium, I offer my apologies for the loss of your men and the damage caused to your equipment and building. You will be compensated. I will take these men into custody and remove them from the premises. Your coopera—"

Several loud cracks interrupted the rest of the Guardian's words. As if all that he had witnessed had not been enough of a shock, Dr. Rana watched in amazement as the Guardian shook convulsively from a dozen laser bolts that shot through his armor. A second later, the man's enormous body fell to the floor, lifeless and still.

Shaking uncontrollably, the Hindu doctor slowly turned his head toward the front of the room. There, standing with weapons pointed at the dead Guardian, were four heavily armored robots. Moving quickly up behind the metal monstrosities were eight men dressed in the garb of the Islamic fighters from the city of Bab al-Jihad.

20

SURPRISES

"Um…hi, Marcel," Raptor said, mustering all the bravado he could to mask his complete shock at the sudden appearance of the other man. "It's so good to see you!"

Marcel's grin widened. "It's good to see you too, you lying sack of *igri* guts. Bind them!" he said to his men.

Knowing that putting up a fight would be pointless, Raptor and Jade didn't resist. While his men placed metallic binders around their wrists, Raptor studied the other man. Marcel had always been physically strong—even a little bit stronger than his brother, Charon. His imposing frame was further enhanced by a *svith* scale jacket similar to the one that Raptor himself was wearing. However, while Raptor's was black with red lines around the edges of the scales, Marcel's was completely blood red and lined with small spikes. Beneath the jacket, the mercenary leader wore a close-fitting, solid white shirt that seemed to be struggling to contain the man's girth. His black pants and boots appeared almost durable enough to stop a laser. Like his brother, Marcel's chiseled features were crowned with a mop of long blond hair. Unlike his brother, who liked to wear his hair loose, Marcel had his coiled into dreadlocks.

With his captives securely bound, Marcel stepped closer to Raptor and Jade. Taking out two Implant Inhibitors from his pocket, he placed one of the small devices on the temples of each of his victims. "There. We don't want either of you calling to my baby brother for help. As much as I'm looking forward to seeing him again, I think I'd like to keep my arrival here a secret. I don't want you to ruin my little surprise."

"Yeah, we wouldn't want that," Raptor replied with obvious sarcasm.

Ignoring the remark, Marcel walked over to the couch that sat in the middle of the office in which they had gathered. Settling into it, he motioned for his men to bring Raptor and Jade closer. As they moved to do his bidding, one of them closed the door of the room.

"So," Marcel began as he chewed on his tobacco stick, "how about I save us all some time and save you the effort of having to come up with some stupid lie about why you're here by giving you my own assessment. Then you can just fill in the blanks for me.

"Based on all the newsfeeds about you and that rogue scientist stealing something from Mathison, and considering that most of the Guardians have followed you to Dehali, I'm guessing that you're well over your head in *crip* dung. You didn't want them to know the location of your *real* base, so you used my old trick of setting up a second false one. You discovered the tracker on your car and so you kept coming here to throw them off the trail. I'm guessing you've found it and removed it by now, right?"

Raptor nodded. "Of course."

Marcel continued. "You also used my idea of setting up hidden sensors to detect if anyone was inside the building before you entered. However, you made two fatal errors.

"Number one, you assumed that Sarbjeet was tracking your movements to give to the Dehali military, not realizing that he actually had no knowledge of it," Marcel continued, enjoying himself immensely. "Do you remember that attractive assistant of his? Yeah, you know the one. Well, as it turns out, Lajvati and I go way back. She recognized you immediately and gave me a call.

"Your second mistake was using the hidden sensors. Of course, to be fair, they were set up for the Dehali military, the ESF, or the Guardians. I'm sure you didn't expect *me* to show up on your doorstep. Really, Rahib, you should have known better than to run from me. You had to have known I'd find you eventually. And if you're going to use my tricks, you should at least tweak them a little. It was way to easy for me to bypass them."

"Thanks for the advice," Raptor commented dryly. "I'll be sure to remember that for next time."

Marcel's smile faded, leaving his expression cold. "There may not *be* a next time if you don't pay me what you owe me."

Raptor rolled his eyes in irritation. "Marcel, you need to expand your vocabulary. I suppose it's a waste of time for me to point out that if anything, you are the one who owes *us!* You lied about the true price of that cargo we picked up on that Nelson deal. Then, we had everything under control when the ESF arrived, but you decided to take a shot at one of them, causing a completely unnecessary confrontation. Not only did we lose most of the payoff, but you withheld our portion of what we *did* manage to come away with then had the *gall* to say that we *owed* you ten thousand credits because we didn't get the whole thing. And on top of all that, you ruthlessly gunned down Collins just to make a point!"

Marcel's lip curled into a sneer. "You're right, you *are* wasting my time. The way I see it, Mathison's put a hefty price on your head that would more than make up for the money you owe me. The only reason why I haven't turned you in already is my curiosity. I want to know why Mathison wants you so bad. Who knows? Maybe if you're story is entertaining enough, and if you give me the money you owe me, I may let you live after all."

The expression on Raptor's face slowly changed from one of defiance to one of defeat. "Look, as you've so eloquently put it, we're over our heads in *gridik* spit right now." Beginning with his meeting Steven, Braedon, and Gunther, Raptor recounted the events of the last two weeks. As he spoke, Jade took note of the fact that he left out all mention of the Vortex weapon, as well as any reference to Steven's prophecy. She also noticed that he seemed to be embellishing other details, making his story take much longer than it should have, almost as if…

Two loud explosions erupted somewhere in the building, shaking the room in which the group had gathered and knocking a couple of Marcel's men off their feet. Cursing, Marcel leapt to his feet even as one of his thugs burst through the door. "We're under attack!" the man yelled in panic. "We're surrounded! They've blown holes in the front and rear of the building!" Even as the words tumbled out of his mouth, the sounds of laser fire and screaming could be heard coming from opposite directions.

"Surrounded? By whom?" Marcel demanded.

"By the Dehali military and…and several Guardians!"

"General Ranjit, our men are in position. What are your orders, sir?"

Ranjit looked up at the giant Guardian leader standing next to him. Fighting to keep the rapid beating of his heart from betraying him, he took a deep breath before speaking. "Prometheus, this is your quarry. How would you like to proceed?"

The bright red lines running between the man's scaly skin flared slightly. "We wait. I have dispatched several of my men to infiltrate the building silently. They will take out the criminals. The ESF agents are in flanking positions. You and your men are to stand by only for support and to clean up afterward."

Using every ounce of inner strength, Ranjit managed to keep his outrage contained. "I understand. Lieutenant, relay the orders. We are to remain in position." *This is it*, Ranjit thought excitedly. Opening up a communications channel via his implant, he contacted his commanders. *All men, I am overriding the instructions you were just given. Activate the Implant Disruptors and be prepared to attack.*

Prometheus stood as still as a statue, his attention focused solely on the readouts and communications he was receiving through his implant feeds. Around him, General Ranjit and several of his men were moving about the restaurant that they had commandeered and converted into a base of operations. His Guardian's were preparing to enter the building. Although he trusted his soldiers to do their jobs with precision, he also knew better than to underestimate his opponents. These criminals were resourceful, and even though he couldn't ignore the lead from the credit stick purchase, he didn't trust it. Something wasn't right here. He could feel it.

The Guardian leader forced himself back to his immediate surroundings. A sudden stillness had permeated the atmosphere. There was tension in the air. It was the feel of men who were about to go into battle. And not just any battle. Even if Ranjit hadn't told them to stand down, the nervousness he sensed was more than what was warranted from just attacking some smugglers. It almost felt like they were preparing themselves to...

The truth of the situation struck him just before the first blaster bolt hit his armor from behind. At the same moment, he felt a wave of nausea overwhelm him. Diving to his left, he crashed into several chairs and a table as more laser fire tracked his movements. His armor absorbed several of the shots, but too many still found their way through. Stabs of pain pierced his body, further adding to his confused state. Thrashing out wildly in panic, Prometheus hurled everything he could find toward his assailants. Although he couldn't tell if his attacks succeeded, there was a momentary lull in the laser fire. Taking advantage of the respite, he placed his feet against the concrete wall and, using his enhanced leg muscles, leapt toward the light filtering in through the front windows. Glass showered over him as he broke through, numerous tiny shards finding their way through the scales on his exposed face.

Landing hard on the pavement, Prometheus shrugged off the fresh waves of pain. Summoning his strength, he climbed slowly to his feet. However, just as he was regaining his balance, a grenade landed behind him. Reacting faster than any normal human could, he leapt upward as the device exploded. The force of the explosion, combined with his own jump sent him sailing into the second story of a nearby building. Fire ripped up his back and legs and peeled away sections of his armor. Letting out a cry of fury, he activated his computer-regulated pain control system. Instant relief flooded over him, allowing him to clear his mind and better assess his situation.

Outside the building, he could hear shouting and sounds of more combat. Although he was out of immediate danger, he knew he wouldn't be safe for long. He would contact his men and, together, destroy these pathetic Dehali soldiers.

However, just as Prometheus prepared to open a communications channel, he realized the sudden truth of why he had felt momentarily blinded and nauseous: his implant connection was no longer functioning. Something was blocking it.

Instantly, the full implications of what had transpired washed over him. The Dehali military had found a way to block implant commands. He was now cut off from his men who were likely being slaughtered before they even knew what hit them, along with the remaining ESF agents. He had to find a way to rescue as many of the other Guardians as possible and get out of this dead zone so he could send a message to Mathison to inform him of this traitorous act. Prometheus snarled. His "master" would probably be pleased. The war he longed for was finally here.

Then, as if hit in the stomach by a powerful blow, Prometheus sucked in a breath in shock as another thought struck him. The Dehali military had the ability to block implant signals from a distance without using the small

Implant Inhibitors. If he could obtain one of the devices used to produce this effect, he would finally have the means to break free of the chains that Mathison had used to enslave him. He had found a way to defeat the kill switch implanted in his heart.

Invigorated with new purpose, Prometheus jumped to his feet and moved further into the building in hopes of finding a way to escape this trap. He would succeed. And when he did, he would hunt down Mathison personally.

21

Army of the Ahmed Caliphate

Gunther opened his eyes slowly, the back of his head throbbing from where he had hit it against the hard tile after the Guardian had tripped him. For a moment, he fought through the haze to try to remember what had happened. However, the moment his eyes fell upon the dead body of the Guardian lying several yards away, his memories returned with powerful clarity. Turning his gaze toward the front of the room, his stomach lurched as he saw several of the Islamic terrorists heading in his direction. Their faces and heads were covered with white *keffiyehs*, or head scarves, and ringed with black headbands, leaving only their eyes visible—eyes that seemed devoid of compassion.

Fear enveloped Gunther in a dark shroud, accompanied by uncontained panic. With his mind engulfed in terror, he forced himself to stand and began moving as quickly as his sore body would allow. But before he even took his second step, strong hands grabbed him and painfully forced his arms behind his back. Turning him around, his captives began dragging him forcibly toward the front of the room. In his fear-induced state of mind, Gunther barely noticed that Travis had been brought along and was being dragged with him by another group of men.

Looming before them were the four robots that had killed the Guardian. However, as he drew nearer to them, Gunther realized that they weren't robots at all, but rather mechanical suits of armor that were being piloted by Islamic soldiers. The heads of each of the mechs nearly scraped the ceiling of the ten-foot-high room. The bulky suits were designed to enhance the movements of the soldiers and were equipped with several types of rockets, missiles, and rapid-fire projectile weapons strapped to the arms and shoulders. Through a thick rectangular sheet of darkened glass about two feet wide on the machine's head, the vague outline of the pilot could be seen. The design of the head made it look like it had its own metallic *keffiyeh*, with the pilot's viewport serving as the eyes.

Gunther was so fixated on the robotic suits that he failed to notice that his captors had brought him to stand in front of what appeared to be their leader. Unlike the others, this man had his *keffiyeh* open, revealing the hardened features of an Arabic man in his early thirties. Gunther barely noticed the common black goatee and dark skin because of the disfiguring four-inch scar that ran from just over his right eye, across the bridge of his nose, and onto his left cheek.

The man began to speak, but it took Gunther several seconds to focus his mind on what was being said. Finally, Dr. Rana's voice penetrated the fog clouding his mind, the words piercing his soul further.

"Greetings, Emir Mofty. I am…I am forever in your debt for your assistance," he stammered, the words coming out in rapid fire. "Your timing was providential! I must confess that I…I was not expecting you. As you can see, you have arrived in the middle of a very unfortunate situation. I apologize, but I don't have any new servants ready for you to take. We had some new arrivals mere moments ago, but have not had time to process them yet. One of them was young and attractive and should make a perfect wife for one of your men. I'm sure if you—"

"Shut up!" the Islamic general snarled. "I'm not here for more chattel at this time. I've come to retrieve a prize for the Imam," he said, his eyes turning toward Gunther and Travis. Reaching up a hand, he found and deactivated the holographic masks that covered their faces.

Dr. Rana's eyebrows rose in surprise. "You…but how do you know these men? And how did you come to know they would be here at this time?"

"We were sent by Imam Ahmed to retrieve them, but we were uncertain where they were hiding. It was by the blessings of Allah that we were given the time and place of their actions." A slight smile creased Mofty's stern gaze as he stared knowingly at Gunther. "You were unwittingly betrayed by one of your own. Yes, one of your foolish friends has an addiction to the technological abomination that you call Pandora's Box. While we abhor the way this satanic tool is used to pervert the mind, we have discovered that it can be a valuable source of information. Many who wallow in the debauchery and technological bliss offered by this unholy tool often forget that it is not real or completely private. Lost in their fantasy worlds, they speak secrets aloud to their imaginary confidants, forgetting that others might be listening. One of the faithful to Allah was stationed at the location your friend visited, and during his session, your dark-haired associate revealed much that should have remained hidden."

Gunther's knees weakened, forcing his captors to hold him upright so that he didn't fall. "Xavier…" he whispered. Beside him, he saw Travis hang his head in hopelessness.

"Yes, that is his name," Mofty said, relishing the power he held over the men. "Allah smiles upon us and delivered you into our hands. And now, you will return with me to Bab al-Jihad, where you will construct for us a copy of this new weapon you have developed and show us how to change the portals so that we may return to earth." The Islamic general's eyes shifted to look at his men standing behind Travis and Gunther. "Grab their equipment and head back to the tunnel."

"What should we do with their companions?"

"Kill them."

"No!" Gunther shouted, his voice raw with emotion.

However, before the men could begin their gruesome task, the faint sounds of approaching footsteps could be heard coming from outside the doors of the room.

"Emir Mofty," Dr. Rana said, a look of sudden concern crossing his face, "when the Guardian attacked, I called for backup for my guards. You must hurry! They cannot find you here or discover the hidden tunnel!"

Gunther's head snapped up in surprise. Looking past the Islamic general, he noticed for the first time that a portion of the back wall had been moved aside to reveal a large tunnel. Remembering what Kianna had said about this facility, he knew that the tunnel led into the back wall of the enormous cavern that housed the city of Dehali.

Mofty's lip curled in frustration. "Indeed. You will tell them that these two intruders must have killed the Guardian and attacked you as well before fleeing."

"Attacked?" Dr. Rana echoed.

"Yes. We don't want anyone to know about our arrangement," he said, then backhanded the doctor. Even before Dr. Rana's unconscious body hit the ground, Taj El-Mofty gave the signal to his men, and they moved quickly into the tunnel and sealed the entrance, taking Gunther and Travis with them.

"Braedon! Braedon are you okay?"

Fighting against the vertigo that resulted from the blow to the head he had suffered when he landed on the floor, Braedon sat up to see Kianna hovering over him. "They… they're gone," he stammered weakly. "They took Gunther and Travis. We have to go after them."

"Slow down. Who took them? What happened?"

Forcing strength into his limbs, Braedon leaned on Kianna and stood. "The Army of the Ahmed Caliphate. They came through the secret tunnel behind that wall," he finished as he pointed toward the front of the room. As he did so, he noticed for the first time that they were not alone. Seven men and women in Dehali military uniforms were moving around the room, assessing the situation. "Wha… what's going on? We've got to get out of here!" he said in a forced whisper.

"Relax. I'll take care of it. I made a fake ID for myself. They believe I'm one of the employees of the Center."

Together, the two of them made their way across the floor to where Xavier lay. Crouching next to him was one of

TARTARUS CHRONICLES BOOK 2: DEHALI

the soldiers from the Dehali military. As they approached, Xavier, who still had his holographic mask in place, sat up. Seeing that he was okay, the soldier stood to address Braedon. "Let's get you some medical attention, then you can tell me what happened in here. Agira, Vrisan, help these two into one of the other rooms. See to it that the building's medical staff treat their wounds."

Nodding, one of them assisted Braedon while the other helped Xavier off the floor. Along with Kianna, the group then headed through the east door of the room and into one of the individual medical rooms, where one of the shaken up staff members began cleaning and bandaging the gash on Braedon's head. With their charges taken care of, the two Dehali military soldiers left to return to the central room.

As soon as the men had gone, Braedon thanked the attending nurse and hurried Kianna and Xavier out into the hallway. "We've got to get out of here now before Dr. Rana wakes up."

Kianna frowned. "What's wrong? What's so important about Dr. Rana waking up?"

"There's no time. I'll fill you in later. Where's Charon?"

Looking around quickly to make sure the coast was clear, Kianna led them down the hall. "I told him to meet us at the side exit. This way."

The three of them hurried as fast as they dared down the busy hallway, doing their best to avoid any wayward glances. Then, with less than ten feet to go before they reached the exit, they heard a shout from behind them. Kianna spun her head around to see four soldiers running toward them down the hall as they reached for their weapons.

"Go!" she said as she nearly pushed Braedon and Xavier toward the door that led out of the building.

Kianna pressed the switch on the wall, causing the door to slide open. Seconds later, a volley of laser bolts struck the wall a foot above the door frame. Diving outside, Kianna, Braedon, and Xavier took cover around the outer wall. A moment later, the automatic door shut.

"Quickly! This way!" Kianna urged, leading the two men along the side of the building toward the parking area.

"We're not going to make it!" Xavier called out. "Those soldiers will be through that door any second!"

Then, to his surprise, the Spelunker veered around the corner of the building and pulled up next to them just as Xavier's prediction came true. Not wasting any time, Kianna, Braedon, and Xavier opened the side door of the hovering vehicle and leapt inside as Charon climbed out of the driver's seat, a large rifle in his hands.

At the sight of the new assailant, the four soldiers raised their weapons and moved quickly back toward the safety of the building entrance. Using the driver's side door as a shield, Charon squeezed the trigger of the Volt, sending a stream of electricity arcing toward the four men. Convulsing, they fell to the ground, unconscious.

Letting out a twisted laugh of victory, Charon tossed the rifle back into the vehicle, climbed inside, and drove off. Moments later, the Spelunker headed onto the main road and sped down the street to become lost in the traffic flow of the city.

22

Exit Strategy

Marcel spun around to face Raptor with barely contained rage. "I should kill you right now! You knew they were following you!"

Raptor met his fury with steely determination. "Hey, it's not my fault that you chose an extremely inopportune time to try to nab me."

Swearing violently, Marcel sent all but four of his men out of the room to join in the fighting. Turning back around, he grabbed Raptor's collar. "But you wouldn't have led them here unless you had an exit strategy. Where's your hidden escape?"

"Down in the basement, there's a hole that leads into the city sewers."

"I thought so." Leaning back, Marcel's eyes lost their focus momentarily as he tried to communicate with the rest of his team. "What the…?" Confused, he turned to look at his men. "Can any of you reach the others?" For several seconds, each of the other four men attempted to use their implants to no avail. Frustrated by the sudden loss of his implant feed, Marcel stared malevolently back at Raptor.

"What kind of game are you playing now, Rahib? How did you manage to block all of our implants? No one has that kind of technology!"

"I'm not doing it, but I have a good idea who is," Raptor replied. "Sarbjeet gave us a little demonstration of the devices the other day. My guess is that the Dehali military are using them to disrupt our communications and prevent us from using our implants to activate any traps or explosives."

Marcel studied Raptor for several seconds, trying to make up his mind on whether or not to believe him. Finally, he turned toward two of his men. "We'll just have to do this the old-fashioned way. Higgins, head to the front, Gage, go to the back. Tell the others to make for the basement exit. Go!" Without pause, the two men ran out of the room.

Once they had left, Marcel moved around behind Raptor and pressed the nozzle of his gun into his captive's back. "Let's go. And unless you want to become worm food like your old buddy Collins, I suggest you warn me in advance of any little 'surprises' you may have hidden along the way."

"Yeah, yeah. I got it," Raptor mumbled as Marcel's muscular arms shoved him out of the office and into the hallway.

With their arms secured in front of them, Jade and Raptor moved rapidly down the corridor with Marcel and the other two men following behind. The cacophony of battle mingled with the shouts and screams of men filtered down the hallway from both directions. Just as the small group reached the door that led to the stairway, an explosion ripped through the building, knocking everyone off their feet. Recovering quickly, Jade kicked the gun out of Marcel's hand. Spinning past him, she threw her left shoulder into one of the other thugs who had just regained his stance. The blow caused him to lose his recently reacquired balance and knocked him backward. However, the maneuver failed to take out the third man, who jumped aside and raised his weapon toward Jade.

Having just recovered from the initial explosion, Raptor watched helplessly as the man prepared to fire. Suddenly, a small shadow detached itself from the ceiling and dropped onto the man's face. Screaming as the furry creature dug its claws into the man's skin, he dropped his weapon and reached up with his hands to remove the small attacker. Reacting immediately, Jade kicked the man in the chest and sent him reeling backward into the wall.

Enraged, Marcel lunged toward Raptor and knocked him to the ground. With his hands bound, Raptor could only manage to keep his elbow up to ward off the fists of the much larger man. After only a few seconds of struggling, Marcel managed to land a blow against Raptor's chin, momentarily stunning him. An instant later, the muscular crime lord had his opponent's throat between his meaty hands.

"I never understood why my idiot brother befriended an Arabic reject like you," Marcel growled as he choked the life out of Raptor. Struggling to breathe, Raptor looked over toward Jade, hoping against hope that she might come to his aid. However, he could see that she was engaged in her own battle with one of Marcel's men. With her hands bound, the martial arts master was forced to resort mostly to kicks. Although he didn't doubt the outcome of the battle, he knew that any help from his friend would be too late.

Then, just as his eyesight was beginning to dim, he heard a crash nearby and suddenly felt the pressure from Marcel's grasp release. Coughing and gasping for air, Raptor rolled over onto his stomach. Gathering his strength, he pushed himself up onto his knees and turned to find out where his attacker had gone.

To his complete surprise, he stared in shock at his unexpected savior. Standing between Raptor and Marcel was a monstrous Type II Guardian. The genetically altered man had a wicked snarl on his dog-like face as he reached forward and grabbed Marcel by the front of his shirt and lifted him off the floor. Frantic, the large man withdrew a hidden knife from concealment and stabbed it into the Guardian's side. Howling in rage, the hybrid hurled Marcel into the wall. The force of the throw sent the crime lord's body through the wall and into the adjoining room, where his broken form lay still and unmoving.

"Raptor, c'mon!" Jade urged as she reached down and pulled her friend to his feet. "We've got to get out of here now!"

Stunned, Raptor glanced down the hallway to see that Jade had indeed succeeded in dispatching both of the men, and her pet *mindim*, Zei was now resting on her shoulder. However, before either of them could move, more gunfire erupted in the hallway. Hunching down next to the wall for protection, Jade and Raptor watched in confusion as a group of Dehali military soldiers opened fire on the Guardian that had just saved Raptor.

The dog-like hybrid's elongated face grimaced in pain as the laser bolts slammed into his armor. Diving toward the hole in the wall made by Marcel's body, he raised his arm and launched a small missile down the hallway just before leaping through the opening. Although the trajectory of the missile was off, the attack succeeded in forcing the soldiers to break off their advance and seek cover.

Then, to Raptor and Jade's increased horror and awe, a dark shape out of their nightmares seem to magically appear out of the smoke from the resulting missile strike. Another Guardian with blood red reptilian scales and twisted horns began striking out at the Dehali soldiers. Bodies flew threw the air as the Titan rampaged through their ranks.

Shaking off the horror of the scene, Jade pulled Raptor through the doorway and into the stairwell. Flying over their heads, Zei chirped noisily as it flew down the stairs to perch on the lowest railing. Closing the door behind them, Jade helped Raptor down the steps toward the basement.

"What…what just…happened back…back there?" he said, his throat still raw and aching from Marcel's grip.

"I don't know," she replied as they reached the bottom. "I thought the Dehali military and the Guardians were working together."

"Yeah, me too. All I know is, I don't care to stick around to ask questions."

"Right. Here. Hold out your hands."

Raptor did as Jade commanded and, to his surprise, found she had picked up a pistol during the scuffle in the hallway. Although she was unable to remove the binders completely, she was at least able to break the metal that kept the binders together.

"C'mon, let's go," Raptor said. "The fighting has stopped upstairs. They'll be coming for us any second." Looking around nervously, Zei chattered rapidly in agreement from its perch on the railing. "Wait a second! I almost forgot!" Reaching into his jacket pocket, Raptor removed the credit sticks he'd withdrawn earlier. "With Marcel's surprise visit, I didn't get a chance to ditch these. A lot of good it would do us to escape only to have them track us down again!"

Jade's eyes widened as she realized how close they'd come to blowing their plans. Pressing the door release, she, Raptor, and Zei leapt through the doorway and into the basement to complete their exit strategy.

"Prometheus, what's going on?" Cerberus asked. He limped out into the hallway of the damaged office building to greet the Guardian leader and the two other Guardians that had saved him from the Dehali soldiers. Behind them, the sounds of battle were beginning to fade.

"We have been betrayed," Prometheus said with a snarl. "We have to escape the city and inform Mathison that General Ranjit opened fire on us. We are all that is left. The rest of our men were ambushed."

"But how will we get out?" Cerberus asked.

"The fugitives have fled down the stairway. They must have an exit down there," the Guardian leader stated. "We'll follow them and complete our original mission. After that, we'll find a way to obtain the devices that our betrayers used to block our implants. Then, we'll return to Elysium and deal with Mathison. With the might of Elysium behind us, we will crush this city and all who oppose us."

"As you command," Cerberus said, a wicked grin spreading across his features as he comprehended the meaning of Prometheus's words.

"Quickly now," Prometheus ordered. "General Ranjit and his men are coming."

Heading down the stairway, the technologically altered hybrid led his men into the basement. Once inside, they came to a sudden halt.

"Where are they?" one of the Guardians asked, his eyes scanning the room for any sign of their quarry.

"They must have a hidden exit. Search the room." Moving into the center or the large storage area filled with tables, chairs, and other unused office equipment, Prometheus cycled his enhanced optical scanner through its various settings. "There!" he called out at last. "Over in that corner, behind those desks, is a hidden doorway concealed by a holographic image."

The Guardians quickly opened a path to the indicated spot. Within seconds, they had disabled the holographic projector and exposed the hidden door. Smiling, Prometheus looked at his men. "Come. Let's continue the hunt. They will not escape!" Although the opening was a tight fit for the large men, within moments, they had disappeared down the ladder that led into the sewers to complete their mission.

23

AFTERSHOCKS

"I think things have finally settled down. Let's get out of here."

Together, Raptor and Jade grabbed onto the handles set into the back side of the secret wall and pulled. With only a little effort, they were able to slide it along its track so that it was out of their way. Stepping out cautiously from the small, hidden room, they moved into the large storage area. In the corner, the once-concealed hole leading to the sewers stood open.

Glancing down at the device in her hand, Jade double-checked the readings from the sensors. "It looks like most of the remaining Dehali soldiers have moved out in the two hours since we went to ground. There are only a dozen or so still left in the building, and most of those seem shaken and distracted. There's no sign of any of the Guardians anywhere."

"Just like we planned it."

Jade snickered. "Right. Except for Marcel showing up, getting our hands bound, the Guardians and Dehali military attacking each other, and almost getting killed, everything went off without a hitch."

"You can't predict everything, you know," Raptor said with a shrug.

"I will hand it to you, though, you did predict that the Guardians would find the hidden tunnel to the sewers and assume we escaped through there, and you predicted that they wouldn't find the hidden room. Good call."

"Yeah," he said with relief. "With all of the technology at their disposal, sometimes it's the non-technological solution that people overlook. Now for the last part. Are you ready?"

Adjusting her Dehali military uniform, Jade pressed her finger to a spot just behind her right ear and activated the holographic mask. The uniforms, which they had hidden in the secret room two days prior, fit perfectly. Within moments, both she and Raptor had the appearance of two average Dehali soldiers.

Reaching down, Jade picked up the satchel that contained their clothes and other tools, including the laser tool they had used to remove their bindings. In addition, the satchel held the sleeping *mindim*. With all of the excitement, Jade was forced to give the small flying rodent a mild sedative to keep it from chattering and giving away their hiding place. Besides, she and Raptor had decided that two soldiers leaving with a *mindim* flying next to them would definitely attract some unwanted attention.

Heading out of the room, they climbed the stairs leading back to the main floor. Once they entered the hallway, they fought to keep from reacting to the shock and horror of their surroundings. The building was in shambles from the numerous explosions and laser fire that had occurred just over two hours ago. Although all the bodies had been removed, there were still bloodstains everywhere.

"Do you think Marcel is dead?" Jade whispered as they walked toward the back exit.

"I don't know," Raptor replied as he studied the damage around them. "That Guardian threw him pretty hard through that wall. If he lived, he's probably in bad shape."

They let the conversation drop as they neared the area where several technicians were still working. Passing unchallenged through the area, Jade and Raptor casually strode away from the building. Once out of the immediate vicinity, they located the recently rented escape vehicle they had parked several blocks away, climbed inside, and breathed deeply.

"Our implants are back online," Jade commented finally. "They must have had the Implant Dampeners focused specifically on the area immediately around the building."

Turning on the computerized driving program, Raptor waited to respond until their car was headed into traffic. "Let's see what the others have been up to. I'll open a dual channel to Charon. Let's hope they got that data."

Immediately, Charon's voice came through their implants, his tone strained and full of irritation. *Where have you been? We've been trying to reach you for hours!*

The Dehali military set up some of those Inhibitor Dampeners in our area, Raptor replied. *We'll fill you in on the details later. First tell me what happened with you. Did Gunther and Travis get the data?*

A feeling of dread seeped into Raptor's stomach and spread throughout his body as Charon filled him in on the situation. *From what Braedon said, Gunther and Travis did get the information they needed, but…somehow…Raptor, you're not going to like this.*

What? What happened? he asked, his blood turning cold.

Your father's men showed up and…they took Gunther and Travis and all of their equipment with them through the secret tunnel.

Raptor felt a sudden dizziness wash over him. For the past several weeks, he had succeeded in pushing the disturbing thoughts of Steven's prophecy from his mind by keeping busy. Everything had been going according to plan, and with those portal readings, Gunther and Travis were supposed to have been able to stabilize the portals from earth. Steven's prophecy gave him thirty-one days to live, and they had done all of this in eighteen days, beating the deadline by almost two full weeks.

But now, everything had changed. Instead of having twelve days to spare, he had only twelve days left to do the impossible. If his father's men had taken Gunther and Travis, it could only mean one thing: he wanted the scientists to give him the technology of the Vortex weapon.

Charon's words interrupted Raptor's thoughts. ***Look, Rahib. You did your best, but it's over now.***

No, it's not!

C'mon! Charon replied, his rage coming through the TC. ***IT'S OVER! You're dad's goons have got the old man and his buddy! Without them, we can't get the Vortex to work.***

Which is why we're going to get them back!

Have you gone insane? They're probably halfway to Bab al-Jihad by now! Charon countered. *Do you have amnesia or something? Don't you remember that you* **vowed** *never to go back there again?*

Really, Caleb? Do you think I needed a reminder of that? But things have changed.

The only thing that's changed is you! Ever since that fool Steven gave you that stupid prophecy, you've lost your flippin' mind.

Open your eyes! This is about way more than just that prophecy! Raptor shot back. *The Guardians and Dehali military were fighting each other! Do you know what that means? It means war between Dehali and Elysium! You know as well as I do that my father has been building his army for years and waiting for a time to strike. Now he has Gunther and Travis and all of their research!*

Yes, but he doesn't have the Vortex weapon, Charon replied. *You still have that hidden safely back at the temple.*

But along with the research were the blueprints for the weapon. With all of his resources and a full team of engineers, it won't take them long to build another one.

But that's not our problem! We can head toward New China or some other territory and lay low. This isn't our war!

For the first time, Jade entered the conversation, surprising both men with her passion. *You're the one with amnesia, Caleb. Don't you remember? Both Sarbjeet and Braedon's friends told us that something is causing Tartarus to become unstable? Don't you remember the earthquake that just happened here and in New China? You obviously remember the svith attack out in the Fringe. These earthquakes are driving them from their nesting grounds. We can't just sit and hide in some hole somewhere. We, all of us, have to either find a way out of Tartarus, or we die.*

Charon remained silent for so long that Raptor began to wonder if they'd lost the connection. *Yeah,* he said at last. *I get it. I just wanted to make sure you weren't doing this because…because of that false prophecy. So what do we do now?*

Raptor looked over at Jade, the muscles in his jaw twitching from the tension in his body. *The first thing we need to do is get out of Dehali. Things are too hot here right now, and we don't even know where those Guardians are. We know that the Titan and three others escaped into the sewers, but there were many more in other areas around the city.*

Kianna says she knows of a place outside the city where we could regroup safely, Charon said. *It's not far from, but she said we wouldn't have to worry about being discovered there.*

Jade cast Raptor a suspicious look. "Another one of her Crimson Liberty safe houses?" she asked aloud.

"Probably," he said before returning to the TC conversation. *Send us the coordinates. Jade and I will swing by the temple and grab the Vortex and the rest of our equipment and supplies, then meet up with you. Be careful leaving the city. Don't forget to use the passcode that Sarbjeet gave us.*

Got it.

Caleb, there's one more thing I need to tell you, Raptor said. *We ran into your brother.*

What? Charon replied in surprise. *What happened?*

He got the jump on Jade and me, but in all of the confusion with the Guardians and Dehali military, we got away. However, one of the Guardians threw him through a wall. He may be dead.

Charon paused for a moment. *Good riddance,* he said at last. *It sounds like he got what he deserved. He's bullied me since we were kids. I'm so glad I came from such a great family,* he said sarcastically.

Yeah, well, I wanted you to know. I'll give you all the details when we arrive.

I can't wait to hear it.

Closing down the connection, Raptor leaned back in his seat. Beside him, Jade stirred.

"Listen, are you…are you sure you're ready for this? Are you ready to go back to Bab al-Jihad?" she asked. "We've all got skeletons in our closets and ghosts from our past. Are you ready to face yours?"

Raptor was silent for a long time before responding. "I guess we'll find out." He had thought so often about the part of Steven's prophecy that referred to his limited number of days that he had forgotten the first part. Now, the words came back to him clearly.

> *You have cursed my name for many years,*
> *And have despised those who bear my name.*
> *Why? Because one you loved chose truth instead of lies,*
> *Life, instead of darkness.*

In his mind, he felt the stirring of memories long buried…*one you loved…* He knew he was not ready to visit that dark place. Yet he had no choice. If he went to Bab al-Jihad, the city of his birth, he knew he would have to face those memories—and the past he had worked so hard to forget.

24

THE UNTOUCHABLES

"Glad to see that the two of you could make it," Charon said as Raptor and Jade stepped out of their car.

Raptor studied their surroundings in disgust. Lifting up the collar of his shirt, he covered his nose and mouth as he approached his friend. "Is this Kianna's idea of a joke? If it is, her timing is terrible. I'm not really in the greatest of moods right now."

Charon frowned. "Nope. This is where she brought us: the city dump."

Before they could say any more, the passenger door of the Spelunker opened, and Kianna climbed out. "Listen," she said, "I know this isn't what you probably had in mind for a place to lay low, but we should be safe here. You may not believe it, but I have friends in the area. They've agreed to help us out."

"Huh," Charon scoffed. "What better place to find a Crimson Liberty group than in the trash heap."

A muscle twitched in Kianna's cheek as she fought to control her frustration. "Braedon and Xavier are both banged up pretty good. They need some medical attention and rest. And from the looks of you two, you could use the same. Now we can stand out here and debate this if you want, or you can let my friends help you. What's it going to be?"

Charon had another snide comment on the tip of his tongue, but after seeing the worn-out expression on Raptor's face, he decided to save it for another time.

"Fine. Let's get this over with," Raptor said, a weariness in his voice. "Lead the way. Jade and I will follow."

With the matter settled, the group dispersed and reentered the vehicles. A moment later, the Spelunker hovered down a pathway that led between two huge mounds of garbage, followed close behind by the Raptor and Jade in their wheeled car.

"We've hidden out in some pretty nasty places before, but why would you ever want to make a permanent hideout in the midst of a bunch of..." Raptor stated. However, as they continued down the filthy road, his voice trailed off at the sight that greeted them, his question left unfinished.

They weren't just entering a small hideout but an entire village.

Lining each side of the road were small huts and dwellings made out of whatever materials the builders could find. Since they didn't have to worry about weather or temperature fluctuations, most of the habitations were little more than walled-off sections of ground amidst the grime of the garbage.

Milling about near the tiny shelters were numerous rodents and groups of the pig-like *igri*, as well as throngs of people in various stages of squalor and sickness. Many of the people appeared so weak that they merely lay beside the road, their eyes roaming listlessly about. Soiled strips of cloth served as clothing and were draped haphazardly over their emaciated bodies. Others could be seen sifting through the garbage while their children played aimlessly nearby. Many more walked down the road, their bare feet shuffling over the uneven ground.

Stunned by the sight, Raptor and Jade remained silent for the remainder of their journey. Several minutes later, they arrived at their destination. Two Hindu men stepped in front of the vehicles and directed the group to pull off the road and park next to a row of actual buildings. From the normal look of the men, Raptor guessed that they were Kianna's contacts or some kind of aid workers, or both. Once the vehicles were parked, Kianna exited the Spelunker and approached the two men. After receiving some small objects from them, she returned and waved for the others to join her. Fighting the stiffness that was already setting in, Raptor and Jade exited the car and crossed over to where the others were gathering.

"Here," Kianna said and handed each of them two small devices. "Put these in your nose. They'll filter out the stench. Also, try to breathe through your nose, not your mouth."

"Well, you were right about one thing," Charon said as he looked around the area. "We shouldn't have to worry about anyone finding us here."

Kianna looked at him, her tone serious. "Unfortunately, most of the citizens of Dehali don't even know this place exists. The military know it's here, but they never come near the area."

"What exactly is this place?" Raptor asked, a sense of uneasiness adding itself to his already dour mood.

"This is the village of the Untouchables," Kianna answered. "In the Hindu caste system, the Untouchables rank even lower than the *Shudras* caste of unskilled workers. They are also called *Dalits*. They are ostracized by society because they perform jobs that many consider unclean. Basically, that means any jobs that deal with dead animals or cleaning up after humans. But those are just the ones who are healthy enough to work. The rest of the village is made up of those left to die."

Charon looked disgusted. "So you and your friends are using these people to hide your activities because you know the government won't come here. I've done some things I'm not proud of, but this…this hits a new low."

Kianna shook her head. "That's not it at all. Crimson Liberty only has a presence here because we bring food and aid to these people since no one else will. C'mon, let's go. They're waiting for us." Turning, Kianna helped Braedon as they headed toward the two men.

As Jade and Xavier followed, Raptor gave Charon a wry look. "It looks like you missed the mark on that one, huh?" Looking skeptical and irritated, Charon shrugged and headed after the others. Giving a soft chuckle, Raptor followed behind.

Their guides led the group into the building on the far left, closest to where they had parked. Inside were rows of cots, each filled with people in various stages of health. They passed through the large common area and headed down a hallway lined with doors on each side. Opening one of the doors, the two men helped Kianna assist Braedon inside. The room was furnished with four sets of bunk beds along the walls and a single dresser. The moment Jade stepped through the door, Zei jumped off her shoulder and took up residence on one of the top bunks, chirping happily.

"It's certainly not the Om Tower," Xavier mumbled. "Then again, after the day we just had, I'd settle for just about anything right now."

Once they were all inside, one of the men turned to face Kianna. "This is the best we could do on such short notice," he said in strongly accented English. "This area of the building is set aside for the use of our personnel. There is a bathroom down the hall to the right. A nurse will be by shortly to attend to your wounds, and we'll have some food brought to the room in an hour or so."

"Thank you, Hiral," Kianna said with a smile. "Please express our gratitude to Mahit and the others." Hiral returned her smile, and a moment later, he and his companion left the room.

"Isn't this cozy," Charon said as he sat down on one of the stiff mattresses.

Kianna fought to maintain her composure in the face of the man's arrogance and rude demeanor. "Don't you even have a shred of decency in you? Don't you understand what my friends went through to make this room available to us? You should at least—"

"Oh, save me the lecture, sister."

Seeing the rage welling within Kianna, Raptor interceded. Stepping over to where Charon sat, he motioned for Jade to join them. "Charon, I want you and Jade to go take a look around. Get a feel for the layout and find the quickest way for us to get out of here, just in case. I don't expect trouble, but I'd rather play it safe."

"Don't you think we should discuss what happened today and what we're going to do next?" Charon asked.

"Not yet," Raptor replied. "I think we'll all be in a better mood for that discussion once we've had some food and rest."

"Fine," Charon said. "At least it gives me something better to do than sit around." Standing up, he strode out the door.

"Nice move," Jade commented. "It's a good thing you broke that up. I was starting to get worried Kianna might beat him up."

"I'm gonna tell him you said that," Raptor replied with a smirk.

"You do, and you're going to find yourself buried in that garbage outside! C'mon, Zei," Jade called. Immediately, the flying rodent leapt down from its perch and landed on her right shoulder just before she exited the room.

"Thank you," Xavier said wearily from where he lay on one of the beds. "I don't know if you've noticed this yet, Raptor, but Charon can be quite annoying at times, especially when you've got a headache."

Raptor grinned and sat down on one of the unoccupied beds. With Braedon resting comfortably, Kianna walked over to the remaining bed and sat down.

Raptor studied her for a moment before speaking. "Kianna, you told us that no one else will help the people in this village. Why not? Doesn't Dehali have government programs to help the poor and needy?"

Kianna shook her head sadly. "No. Hindus don't generally practice charity because they feel it would interfere with the law of karma. Although some teach that people should help the poor to build up good karma, many feel that the reason for poverty is because the poor are facing the consequences for their bad actions in a previous life."

Raptor was silent a moment before responding. "So why is Crimson Liberty involved? Why would Christians help a bunch of Hindus?"

Kianna looked at Raptor intently. "One of the most important issues in life is what it means to be human. For a Christian, the answer is simple: we are created by God in his image, therefore *all* life is sacred. We bear the stamp of our divine Maker. This includes the deformed, handicapped, weak, and even those who don't have the same beliefs. This is one of the reasons why Crimson Liberty is against the Guardian program. It devalues human life.

"Unfortunately, other belief systems don't feel the same way," Kianna continued. "Hindus don't want to go against karma, so they don't help the poor, Buddhists teach that life is an illusion, so these people should just meditate to escape from the illusion of suffering, and atheists feel that the poor are a drain on society's resources and should be wiped out."

"I disagree. I've known many atheists who have helped the poor and have done good deeds," Raptor countered. "You sound pretty self-righteous."

"You misunderstand," Kianna said quickly. "I didn't mean to imply that people with other beliefs can't do good. What I'm saying is that, based on their beliefs, they don't have any logical justification for doing so. They might help someone because it *feels* right, but if they dig deeper into their beliefs, they'd realize that they are actually acting *contrary* to what they believe. When secularists help people, they're acting opposite to their beliefs. And if you study the teachings of Christianity, you'd understand that if Christians *don't* help the poor, they are also acting opposite to their beliefs."

"Do all Christians have the same beliefs?" Raptor challenged. "From what I've heard, there are lots of different brands of Christianity out there."

"The core teachings of Christianity are very clear," Kianna countered. "Those who say otherwise either haven't read the Bible themselves or are deliberately trying to twist things for their own purposes."

Raptor looked unconvinced. "Even still, according to Christian teachers, aren't the people in this village just getting what they deserve because they're rejecting your God?"

"You're missing a major point," Kianna replied. "The Bible teaches that *all* humans are sinful, so we're no better than anyone else. Since Jesus forgave us and took away our sins, we should tell others so that they can also find that salvation. Despite what you may think, we don't force our beliefs on people. Instead, we hope to win them over with love, and with truth. One of the unique things about Christianity is that it isn't right *actions* that bring salvation, but rather right *belief*. It is believing that Jesus died for your sins. All the other religions focus on *doing* the right things or following the right rituals."

A sudden knock at the door intruded upon the conversation. Kianna stood and opened it. A nurse entered with a cart full of bandages and other medical supplies. As the woman began cleaning the wound on Braedon's forehead, Raptor stood. "Kianna, you and Braedon may be idealists, but at least you've both done your homework. I'm gonna go inspect the vehicles. I'll be back in about an hour."

Not knowing what else to say, Kianna merely watched in contemplative silence as Raptor left the room and closed the door behind him.

25

REVELATIONS

As promised, Raptor returned an hour later along with Charon and Jade. When everyone had gathered in the room, they ate and related all that had transpired that day. With very little discussion, they all, including a reluctant Charon, agreed that they would leave at the beginning of the waking cycle and attempt to rescue Gunther and Travis from Bab al-Jihad. Kianna also made arrangements for one of her friends to return the rented car that Raptor and Jade had used. Once their meeting was finished, they allowed their exhausted bodies to get some much-needed rest.

Despite his weariness, Raptor slept fitfully and was jolted awake by the same nightmare that had plagued him for weeks. The same nightmare that Steven had accurately described back in Elysium and attributed to God. Closing his eyes, he could vividly see in his mind's eye every detail of the dream. The darkness of the cavern. The horrible sounds of the creature hunting him. The unbearable light coming from a jeweled sword that he couldn't touch. The laughter of the dragon, and the terrifying sensation of being eaten by it.

Unable to return to sleep, Raptor climbed out of bed, threw on his *svith*-scale jacket and went out to where the Spelunker was parked. Climbing inside, he pulled out his holographic reader and activated Steven's journal.

> We shouldn't act upon every urge. Often, physical desires are wrong. Just because we want something physically doesn't mean we should have it, i.e., food, sex, drugs, etc. But why? If we're just evolved animals, then shouldn't we indulge our desires? What would be the social consequences of that philosophy?
>
> But we are more than just animals. God didn't give us moral laws as stifling rules to repress and restrict us, but as directions for how to become the kind of being he intended for us to be. To ignore known physical laws like gravity is the height of folly, just as ignoring God's moral laws will always have painful consequences.
>
> In addition, the very existence of these physical desires points toward God's existence. Let me explain. The reason we hunger is because there is such a thing as food. We thirst because there is water. We desire intimacy because there is love. Yet within each of us is a longing, a desire for something greater than ourselves. As C. S. Lewis put it in his book, *Mere Christianity*, "If I find in myself desires which nothing in this world can satisfy, the only logical explanation is that I was made for another world."

Raptor paused in his reading, a sense of unease coming over him. Despite his best efforts to convince himself otherwise, he knew that Steven's words had perfectly described what he had felt all of his life. He *did* long for something more, some greater meaning to his life. However, he had always told himself that evolution explained human existence, and that the only meaning he could get from life is what he gave it. Uncomfortable with his own thoughts, Raptor skipped to another entry and began reading.

My sons, you always have the right to your beliefs, but your beliefs may not be right. You have to seek out the truth. Give it thought. Don't just accept what people tell you. Remember, the test of any worldview is if it conforms to reality. Does it match the way things really are?

Faith is not blind. It is based on experience and reason. When you encounter something new that you are unsure of, check it with those things that you are convinced are true. If you are asked to sit in a chair that you've never sat in before, would you have faith that that chair will hold your weight? Yes. Why? Because you've had experience sitting in similar chairs. It is the same with religion. You believe things you may not fully understand because you have come to trust many other things that have been proven. Your past experience gives you the faith to trust in what you don't completely know.

Once you determine your core beliefs, everything else falls into place. There will always be things that you can't prove or don't understand, but as long as it doesn't contradict your core beliefs, you can have faith that it is true. If you had a friend who never lied to you and that friend told you something you couldn't verify, would you believe it? Of course, because he had proven himself trustworthy in the past.

So discovering your core beliefs are crucial to your worldview. That's why I've put so much emphasis on it in this journal. Famous apologist Lee

Strobal once wrote, "Faith is taking a step in the same direction as the evidence is pointing."

Why then do I believe Christianity is true? Why do I place my trust and faith in the teachings of Christianity? Because, when you examine them objectively, you will find it is based on rational propositions and is supported by reason and evidence.

Over the next several entries, I will discuss key ways in which Christianity is unique among the world religions. Please consider these points carefully and do your own research to confirm their veracity.

Christianity contains numerous prophecies.

Imagine if two mechanics were giving you contradictory advice on how to fix the hover actuators on your car. The first one wrongly identifies the part and gives vague instructions, but the second promptly explains step by step how to do the repair. Whose advice would you trust? The second mechanic clearly demonstrated his knowledge.

Now apply this to religion. Many religions make claims about God and the supernatural. Although other religions may have prophecies, none are 100 percent accurate. Which religious text will you trust: ones that make claims only, or the one that supports that claim by including knowledge that only God could have?

Raptor continued to read for several more minutes. He was so focused on the text that he didn't notice Jade's approach until she opened the driver's door and climbed in. "I saw you got up. When you didn't return, I decided to come check on you. The same nightmare again?"

"Yeah."

Knowing from past experience that Raptor didn't want to discuss it, Jade changed the topic. "What are you reading? Anything good?"

Raptor looked down at his reader with conflicted thoughts. Since receiving Steven's journal, he mostly kept its contents to himself. However, due to recent events, he knew he needed to talk to someone. Braedon and Kianna were out, Xavier avoided serious conversations like they were contagious diseases, and Charon was hostile toward religion. Deciding that it was Jade or no one, he cleared his throat. "Before he died, Steven gave me the journal he wrote to his sons in hopes of convincing them that Christianity is the truth. I've been reading it from time to time, and it's been giving me a lot to think about."

Jade's eyebrows raised in obvious surprise. "Really? I've never known you to be overly interested in religion. In fact, you've always seemed pretty set against it. What could Steven possibly have written to change that?"

"There's a lot here," Raptor replied. "Steven was just talking about prophecy in the Bible. He used an analogy that got me thinking about something that happened just a few days ago. See what you think of this. Remember when Sarbeet gave us instructions to meet his supplier?"

"Yeah."

"They were very detailed. He gave us the address, he told us to use the name 'The Brigadier,' he gave us the special code phrase, and we had to pull up to the exact loading bay that Sarbjeet told us. If we failed any of those instructions, we wouldn't have been given the equipment. What do you think the odds would be of someone else getting our order by mistake?"

Jade chuckled. "Almost zero. There are too many requirements that had to be met. But what does this have to do with religion?"

"Well, as it turns out, this is exactly what happened with the prophecies in the Bible about the messiah. Now, I haven't checked Steven's data, but if what he says here is true, it really gives you something to think about. He says that the odds of Jesus accidentally fulfilling just eight prophecies is"—he paused as he referenced Steven's journal—"1×10^{17}. To put that into perspective, he quotes some statistician from Earth. The guy equates it to marking one silver coin, taking the state of Texas from the US—which is about the size of all of Tartarus according to Steven's notes—and covering it two feet deep in the same kind of coin, blindfolding someone and giving them *one* chance to find the marked coin."

Jade's expression became more serious as she realized the scope of what Raptor was saying. "That's impossible."

Raptor nodded. "But that's not even the real kicker. As impossible as that scenario is, it just describes the odds of Jesus fulfilling *eight* prophecies by chance. Yet Steven says that there are over *three hundred* prophecies about the Jewish messiah that Jesus fulfilled!"

Jade narrowed her eyes in disbelief. "Okay, but what kinds of prophecies were they? I've heard a lot of wackos make prophecies, but they're usually extremely vague, leaving the 'prophets' lots of room to explain them away when they don't come true."

Raptor turned the holographic display toward Jade. "See for yourself. Steven lists over twenty of them right here. They are all very specific."

She studied the data for several seconds, her expression revealing her conflicting emotions of skepticism and shock, even fear. Finally, she leaned back away from the reader and shook her head slowly. "Now I see why you find that journal so intriguing. I'd be curious to check his facts. I don't see how they could possibly be accurate."

Shrugging, Raptor gave her a lopsided grin. "Be my guest. I'll make a copy of the journal for you. There are a lot of other things in here that will get you thinking. I'm not sure what to make of it all yet, but it would certainly be nice to have someone else along for the ride."

"Yeah," Jade said. "Hey, speaking of rides, we should probably get moving. The others will be up soon, and we need to get on the road."

Shutting off the holographic reader, Raptor tucked it away in one of his pockets. "Right," he said, his voice distant. Lost in his own thoughts, he opened the door and exited the Spelunker.

Together, he and Jade went back inside and found the others beginning to wake. Within an hour, they had eaten, thanked their hosts, and loaded the Spelunker. During the final preparations, Xavier waited until Raptor, Charon and Jade were occupied before pulling Braedon aside.

"Hey, I...uh...I just wanted to...to thank you," Xavier said awkwardly.

Braedon frowned, confused by the man's out-of-character behavior. "Thank me? For what?"

"Look, I know you were awake back in the Dehali Welcome Center, and I know that you heard what that guy said about how they found us. I...I owe you one for not telling Raptor about...about my Pandora's Box screwup."

Braedon's face darkened in sudden understanding. "Oh. That. Well, I'd be lying if I told you that I'm not angry with you myself. I mean, we wouldn't even be in this situation if it weren't for you. Your mistake could cost the lives of countless people. You get that, right?"

In all the time Braedon had known Xavier, never had the man looked so downcast and miserable. "Yeah, I get it. I've done some stupid stuff in my life, but this one is at the top of the list. It's just that…when I'm in the Box, I just… I just get…lost in it. It won't happen again, though. And please, don't tell Raptor."

"I won't," Braedon promised. "I don't think he'd be quite as forgiving as I am."

Xavier chuckled lightly. "Yeah. I don't think so either."

Finished with the conversation, Braedon stepped passed Xavier and climbed into the back of the Spelunker. Before long, the rest of the group was loaded, and they headed out of the village of the Untouchables.

As the Spelunker left the city of Dehali far in the distance, Braedon made sure the others weren't listening then leaned toward Kianna, who was sitting next to him studying a holographic screen intently.

"Kianna, I've got to tell you something."

Taken off guard by his whisper, she frowned and gave him her full attention. "Is everything okay?"

"Something dawned on me as I listened to the jihadists talk to Dr. Rana," he said. "They said they were sent by Imam Ahmed, who is the governor of Bab al-Jihad, right?"

"Yeah. So."

"Well, when Sarbjeet's servant came to get Raptor from the guest room of the mansion, she called him Mr. Ahmed."

"What?" Kianna said, a little too loudly. Recognizing her error, she shot a quick glance toward the others in the front of the vehicle. Thankful they hadn't heard, she lowered her voice back down to a whisper. "Do you think they're related?"

Braedon shrugged. "I'm not sure, but based on his age and features, I think it's very possible he could be the Imam's son."

Kianna was stunned by the idea. "What does that mean for us? Do you think he's going to turn us in?"

"I don't think so. He's had plenty of opportunities to do that if he'd wanted to. I just thought you should know so that you could keep your eyes and ears open. I'll let you get back to your work. What are you reading anyway?"

Still disturbed by Braedon's revelation, it took Kianna a moment to realize she still had her holographic screen in front of her. "Right. This is a list. When I hacked into the Welcome Center's computer, I was able to retrieve some information on their human trafficking scheme. It appears that our 'friend' Dr. Rana has an ongoing deal with the terrorist group in Bab al-Jihad. Whenever newcomers arrive through the portals, he and his people sedate them immediately. Then, if any meet a certain criteria—namely, females between the ages of twelve and twenty-five—he keeps them held in a special room until they are…sold to the terrorists. The other newcomers are told that the women didn't come through the portal with them. They use that secret tunnel to keep their activities hidden from the general populace. The whole thing just sickens me."

A scowl crossed Braedon's features. "Now I see why your branch of Crimson Liberty was so interested in taking them down. How many have been sold that way?"

"According to this list…over three hundred in the past ten years alone. These are their names and the date they arrived…" Kianna's voice trailed off as Braedon's face paled noticeably. "What is it? What's wrong?"

Braedon swallowed hard as he struggled to find his voice. "You…you said that when newcomers arrive through the portals, sometimes the women are sold and their…companions aren't even aware that they came through the portal with them."

"Yes, that's right," Kianna confirmed, a deep frown creasing her brow.

Braedon stared at her intensely, his eyes filled with fear. "Don't you remember what I told you and Manoj? Let me see that list!" Grabbing the device from Kianna's hand, he began searching the holographic list frantically.

Suddenly, his expression morphed into a mask of horror and grief, causing a wave of concern and dread to pass through Kianna. "Braedon, talk to me!" For several seconds, he remained frozen in place. Finally, Kianna had to shake him to get him to snap out of his stupor.

"Oh, God," he said at last. "Oh, God, no." Numb, Braedon moved his hand and pointed at one of the names on the list of trafficked victims.

"Catrina Lewis," Kianna read the name. "Do you know her? Is she a friend?"

Tears of grief fell down Braedon's cheeks as he answered, his voice raspy and hollow, "Yes. I can't believe…she's been here all along. Ten years and I…I never knew. I have to find her!"

"Who? Who is she?"

"My wife…"

AFTERWORD

Religion and politics. People often state that you shouldn't talk about these two topics in polite company. However, these are *the* two most important topics to discuss. One deals with who we are and how we should act, the other sets the laws and guidelines for encouraging that behavior. Because they are so fundamental to any society, they are at the root of human beliefs and therefore create great passion in many people. And where there is passion, there is bound to be heated conversation. This is why many avoid discussions about religion and politics when in social settings.

But the mistake that many people make is to not delve into the issues at all. They hear some vague illogical statement like, "All religions teach basically the same thing" and believe that as gospel truth without ever thinking it through. Then, when someone tries to make a logical argument for Christianity, they pull out this trump card.

In reality, the statement that "all religions are equal" is simply untrue. As Christian apologist Ravi Zacharias is fond of saying, many people think that all religions are fundamentally similar and superficially different, but in reality, they are *superficially* similar and *fundamentally* different.

Even though people have vastly different beliefs, the real problem lies in the fact that many don't know how to discuss a passionate topic without allowing their passions cause them to lose their civility. It is very possible to have a debate about religion without attacking the other person or their beliefs.

With all of that said, my hope is that I succeeded in doing that in this novel. I prayer is that you, as the reader, were able to perhaps learn a thing or two about Hinduism and Buddhism without the sense that I was attacking those who hold those beliefs. In addition, I also attempted to present some of the logical reasons for belief in Christianity. My goal is to continue to present these arguments in the hopes of *persuading* you.

The Truth Filter

In *Elysium*: Book One of the Tartarus Chronicles, I set the groundwork for examining the truth claims of the various religions. Like a scientist or juror in a court case, we need to (1) Gather Information, (2) Examine the Data, and (3) Draw Conclusions. This information and data should include: eyewitness accounts, historical evidence, archeological evidence, and personal observation (Does it match reality?). In the case of religions, the information that we need to focus on involves the answers to four main questions that each worldview attempts to answer: Where did we come from? (Origin). Why is there pain and suffering? (Evil). What is the purpose of life? (Meaning). What's going to happen when we die? (Destiny).

Furthermore, like a juror, we should examine the witnesses—in this case, the founder of the religion and the written works on which the religion is based. We should consider the backgrounds and possible motives of the founders, as well as how the holy writings of that religion came to be. How and why did they create the religion? What authority do they have to speak about these spiritual topics? When were the holy writings written and compiled? Who wrote them? Are there historical ways to confirm anything written in the books?

In Dehali, I tried to accurately present how Hinduism and Buddhism respond to some of these basic questions and yet do so in a respectful way. In book three, Bab al-Jihad, I will delve into the monotheistic religions of Islam, Judaism and Mormonism.

The Uniqueness of the Bible

In addition to presenting the beliefs of other religions, I am also attempting to show not only how Christianity answers these questions, but also why I believe that Christianity is reasonable and makes the most sense of reality. In Dehali, I brought up a couple of the ways in which Christianity is unique. It is difficult to present information directly in the story without slowing down the pace. So I'd like to use the rest of this Afterword to expound on the two main points I presented earlier.

The first was mentioned by Braedon in chapter 6: the uniqueness of the Bible.

• The Bible is comprised of 66 separate books, and it was written over a period of at least 1,500 years by more than 40 authors who, for the most part, didn't know each other personally.

• The writers of the Bible came from different social and occupational backgrounds (for example Moses, political leader, educated in Pharaoh's palace; Joshua, general;

Solomon, king; Amos, shepherd; Nehemiah, cup-bearer; Daniel, politician; Peter, fisherman; Luke, physician; Matthew, tax collector).

• The authors of the Bible wrote in completely different geographic environments and under different circumstances (for example Moses, in the desert; Jeremiah, in a prison; David, in the mountains and in his palace; Paul, in prison; Luke, during his journeys; John, during his exile on Patmos).

• The Bible was composed on three different continents (Asia, Africa, and Europe) and in three languages (Hebrew, Aramaic, and Greek).

Yet despite all of this, the Bible tells one consistent story of the fall and redemption of mankind that is based in a historically verifiable context. When you examine the writings of the other religions, none even come close. I would encourage you to examine this for yourself.

The Uniqueness of Christianity: Prophecy

The second proof was discussed by Jade and Raptor in chapter 25: prophecy. In that chapter, Raptor read some statistics about Jesus fulfilling prophecies in the Old Testament. Here are five of the most powerful prophecies that Jesus fulfilled. I have included the references in the Old Testament as well as the references for the fulfillment of the prophecy in the New Testament.

Prophecy	Where given	Where fulfilled
Born in Bethlehem	Micah 5:2	Matthew 2:1
		Luke 2:4–6

Betrayed	Psalm 41:9	Luke 22:47–48
	Zechariah 11:12–13	Matthew 26:14–16
Hands and feet pierced	Psalm 22:16	John 20:25–27
	Zechariah 12:10	
Bones not broken	Exodus 12:46	John 19:33–36
	Psalm 34:20	
Soldiers gamble for clothes	Psalm 22:18	Luke 23:34
	Matthew 27:35–36	

Isaiah 53 alone is shocking to read in that it paints a vivid portrayal of Jesus's suffering. The Bible proves its inspiration and authority by offering information that could only come from God.

There are several other ways in which Christianity is unique, but I will discuss those in the next novel.

Your Choice

Reader, please don't just take my word on these points. If you do your own research, I am convinced that you will also realize that Christianity is indeed the truth. Jesus was more than just a teacher. He was the son of God, and his death brought about our salvation. Christianity isn't a religion of dos and don'ts, but a relationship with the God who paid the price for our sin.

It is my sincerest hope that if you have not already done so, you will place your faith in him and accept the free gift of salvation.

SUGGESTED RESOURCES

Books

The Case for Christ by Lee Strobel
The Case for Faith by Lee Strobel
The Case for a Creator by Lee Strobel
Evidence That Demands a Verdict by Josh McDowell
World Religions in a Nutshell by Ray Comfort

Websites

www.apologeticsfiction.com: The official website for Keith A. Robinson.

www.apologetics315.com: A great hub listing other apologetics websites, podcasts and articles.

www.probe.org: The website for Probe ministries. Full of great articles and materials.

www.leestrobel.com: The official website for Lee Strobel. Also full of great videos, articles, etc.

www.answersingenesis.com: Although this website has mostly articles that deal with creation or evolution, there are many other great videos and articles available on a variety of topics regarding Christianity.

www.livingwaters.com: The website for Ray Comfort and Kirk Cameron's ministry.

ABOUT KEITH A. ROBINSON

AUTHOR OF *THE ORIGINS TRILOGY* AND *THE TARTARUS CHRONICLES*

Keith Robinson has dedicated his life to teaching others how to defend the Christian faith. Since the release of *Logic's End*, his first novel, he has been a featured speaker at Christian music festivals, homeschool conventions, apologetics seminars, and churches, as well as appearing as a guest on numerous radio shows.

Since completing his Origins Trilogy, Mr. Robinson has been working on *The Tartarus Chronicles*, a new series of action/adventure novels dealing with the topic of world religions and worldviews.

When not writing or speaking, Mr. Robinson is the full-time public school orchestra director at the Kenosha School of Technology Enhanced Curriculum, and he is a professional freelance violist and violinist in the Southeastern Wisconsin/ Northeastern Illinois area. He currently resides in Kenosha, Wisconsin, with his wife, Stephanie, their five children, and a Rottweiler named Thor.

For more information, visit www.ApologeticsFiction.com.

65136396R00124

Made in the USA
Columbia, SC
13 July 2019